Six Old Women
and
Other Stories

Novels by Sharon L. Dean

DEBORAH STRONG MYSTERIES:

The Barn

The Wicked Bible

Calderwood Cove

Six Old Women
and
Other Stories

SHARON L. DEAN

Encircle Publication
Farmington, Maine, U.S.A.

Editor: Cynthia Brackett-Vincent

Cover design by Deirdre Wait
Cover images © Getty Images

Published by:

Encircle Publications
PO Box 187
Farmington, ME 04938

http://encirclepub.com
info@encirclepub.com

For Ron

In Memoriam

Contents

Introduction

EVERY FEW YEARS, I visit with the women who were my college roommates. We joke that when we're old, we'll winterize the summer houses two of them own, hire a nurse, and live together in our own private commune. That joke provided the germ for *Six Old Women*. My roommates and I aren't ninety yet, and our lives aren't the lives of my characters. But I'm indebted to them for our years of friendship.

Like *Six Old Women*, the stories in this collection are all memory pieces, set in a New Hampshire whose landscape I know well. Although the island in the title novella is fictional, I've spent many days on the shores of Lake Winnipesaukee. The setting for "Shuffleboard" came from my memory of vacationing as a teenager on Newfound Lake, where we loved not only to swim, but also to play shuffleboard. I've skied many times on Cannon Mountain and the trail in my story "Hardscrabble." "Pavlov's Puppies" and "The Man Who Loved Cribbage" come from memories of houses where recluses lived, one covered in gypsy moths during a summer invasion, and one where an old man lived off the grid in the woods.

The characters in these stories all keep secrets. They are as tough and rugged as New Hampshire's iconic Old Man in the Mountain. But like The Old Man who fell in 2003, the pasts I created for them survive only in memory. Sometimes, that's a good thing.

Six Old Women

THEY HIRED ME as a nurse. Six old women living on an otherwise uninhabited island in the middle of Lake Winnipesaukee. The house was huge and shingled, dark and solitary. Five bedrooms, I soon learned, with a sleeping porch off the master bedroom. If I wanted the job, I'd live in the guest cottage that was set behind one of the mounds of earth left from some million-year-old glacial force that shaped New Hampshire's largest lake. A stand of maples and pines hid the guest cottage from the main house.

"Our guests liked privacy," Dottie said when we got out of the boat she'd driven to the mainland to pick me up. The way she said it made me think the "our" was her dead husband and the "guests" were the women I was supposed to take care of. "Don't need a cook," she'd added, though I hadn't asked. "We might all be ninety-two, but we can still broil a trout."

She explained the "we." They'd graduated from UNH,

class of 1950, and had been gathering on Heron Island every summer since then. Years ago, they'd decided that when they were all divorced or widowed, they'd hire a nurse and a handyman and create an island commune for the aged.

"We call this Heron Haven. Can't call it a nursing home," she said. She described the life they'd created since they moved in when they all turned ninety. How they exercised to a DVD every day, took walks around the island, and would swim until September in the cold waters of the lake.

When she tied the boat to the dock, I could see that she was out of breath. Her neck curved forward accenting her cervical thoracic junction. In nursing school we called it the dowager's hump. The flesh on her arms jiggled the way it does when old people lose the collagen beneath their skin. She didn't try to hide it, didn't wear long sleeves or long pants to cover the veins in her legs. Her face looked younger than her body, one of those full round faces that stave off wrinkles that invade the faces of the skinny. She must once have been beautiful.

"Don't need a nurse yet," she said. "At least I don't. I'm a little worried about Stella. She's the skinny one. Better to hire you now than later when we're all on the last train to glory."

We'd been in the boat for less than half an hour. Had she already decided that I'd do? I knew that I wanted the job. Fresh out of nursing school and a year in Boston tending to waning numbers of Covid patients, I thought this would be an easy gig.

She waved her hand around the property. "We need a handyman, too. Or a handywoman. White, brown, black. Doesn't matter." She was declaring herself a woman of the twenty-first century. "You'd have to share the cottage. There are two bedrooms in it. 'Less your husband's interested." She'd nodded toward my wedding ring. "Long as you're not one of those lesbian women." Her tolerance drew a line.

It took me a moment to decide how to answer. "Actually I can't take the job unless you also hire my husband. Richard."

She hesitated as if she were deciding. "Doc Savage recommended only you. Hell of a name for a doctor, but he's a good one. Guess you know him from that Boston hospital he helped out at when we had to shelter from all that Covid stuff. No problem here. We stayed on the island. Had Stewie from the marina deliver our groceries and mail. Is this husband of yours handy? Or is he one of those office types who can't unclog a toilet?"

"He's handy. And he needs the job." I told her about Richard, who'd lost his position as a chef when so many of Boston's high-end restaurants closed.

"Don't need a cook. Did I already say that?"

"You did."

"We need a handyman. Is he as young as you? You look like a teenager. A tiny one at that."

"We're both twenty-four."

"Married young for these days. There's no baby is there?"

"Just us. Richard grew up on a farm where he learned to repair most anything. Leaks, faucets, motors. He can haul wood, till a garden, paint." I made him sound better than he'd shown me since we married.

"Can he drive a boat?"

"He can learn."

"Good. I trust Doc Savage. What's your name again?"

She was sharper than she let on, but I accepted her pretense.

"Nataki Anderson."

"Nataki. Never heard it. You're American, aren't you?"

"Born in Cambridge. The name means 'of royal birth.'" I resisted telling her that I'd been named for the Swahili mid-wife who helped my mother through a difficult labor. She always told me that my birth might not have been royal but it was miraculous. If she'd been able to conceive another child, she would have searched for the mid-wife.

"I'll forgive you for being from Massachusetts. Too many tourists invading our state. Job's yours if you want it. Your husband, too. If we don't like him, we'll dismiss you both."

Richard and I arrived on July first with everything we needed for a long stay on an island where the seasons would move from the humidity of summer into the iced-in days of winter. I knew there'd be weeks when the ice was too thick for the boat to take to the mainland and too thin for the snowmobile that we saw parked among the trees when we carried our things to the cottage. If I needed more than the bandages and sutures and painkillers in my medical kit, I hoped we could get a helicopter to the dock.

Our introductions happened over grilled hamburgers. A salad came from the garden of raised beds that occupied a cleared space on the eastern exposure of the island. I searched for a mnemonic device to help me remember the names of six white women in their nineties. I did a quick calculation. Five hundred and fifty-two years. More if a couple of them had celebrated a ninety-third birthday. I concentrated on their first names. Last names could come later. Except for Dottie Edwards because Richard and I signed a contract with her.

Stella was, like Dottie told me at what passed for an interview, the skinny one. I doubted if her weight was as high as her age. Her spine was curved as much from scoliosis as osteoporosis. Stella, skinny and stooped. I could remember that.

Lucy stood the straightest of the six women and the only one without glasses. She carried herself with an air of privilege, maybe because of the huge diamond she wore on each of her hands. Her nails were polished, her hair dyed to keep its chestnut color free of gray. Lucy in the Sky with Diamonds.

Taller than Stella and shorter than Lucy, Thelma had the thickened waist that came with menopause and hung on as she aged. She'd be Thick Thelma with thick hair. It was a kind of silver that must have come early and that she wore in a natural cut that waved in the humidity. It made me wonder if I'd inherit the job of taking these women to a beauty parlor in Wolfeboro.

Jane was exactly like her name. Plain Jane. Medium height, medium weight, brown eyes behind glasses with brown frames and hair the kind of drab gray that made her look like thousands of other old women. I could see her sense of humor when she smiled at Dottie and called her their house mother.

Dottie introduced Barb as a poet. She'd be easy to remember. Barb the Bard with so many wrinkles on her face they reminded me of lines of poetry.

I had them all fixed in my memory by the time we finished dinner and Dottie announced that she'd tour me through the house. When Richard stood up to follow us, she said, "Not you. Just Nataki."

We walked to the side of the house and into the kitchen. She pointed to a closed door. "Guest bathroom. Not that we have guests. It's just a sink and toilet. We all share the upstairs bathroom. I had to make a schedule for who showers when. I bought different color towels for everyone so they won't mix them up."

I wasn't surprised that Jane called her the house mother. Dottie was the boss. After all, she owned the house.

She waved her arm around the kitchen. "Will Richard approve? Not that we need a cook."

"He would," I said, thinking she insisted too much about not needing a cook. The kitchen would be too sparse for Richard who was used to a high-end restaurant. But it was nice. Light streamed through a window over the sink onto a wooden counter with plenty of space for toaster, microwave, coffee pot, and pottery jars for flour and sugar. The appliances were old and white and wiped almost clean.

"How'd he get that scar? Is he a fighter?"

Richard's scar was what first attracted me to him. It made him stand out from other tanned and muscular men who populated the grounds around U Mass. His sandy hair curled along his forehead and skimmed the edge of an inch-long scar at his temple. I imagined some kind of exotic accident until he told me what happened. "No fighting. When he was a teenager on the farm he tripped on a rake. He was lucky it just missed his eye."

"That's fortunate. His eyes are Paul Newman blue."

I wondered if these six old women were all going to flirt with my husband.

She walked me into the dining room that opened from the kitchen. The table was long enough for eight people. Six placemats marked a color that was coded for each of the women.

Another door opened in a straight line from the kitchen and dining room. Six folding chairs were lined up in front of a television. They had padded seats, but they didn't look comfortable. "That's our exercise room. You'll get to watch us tomorrow."

A third door to the left of the dining room brought us into a large living room with comfortable furniture and another television. A fireplace was cleaned out for the summer, an arrangement of birch logs decorating the interior. Cobwebs hung from the logs.

I followed Dottie up a staircase at the end of the living room. It was uncarpeted and in need of a good mopping. She held onto the banister. To my right at the top of the stairs, a door was closed to a room that must have been above the kitchen. A framed sign on it identified the room as Thelma's. Someone had drawn a caricature of her. Dottie straightened the sign. "Lucy's the artist."

I looked along the hallway. Similar signs marked the other rooms. Dottie and Barb on the right, Lucy and Jane on the left. At the end, I could see a bathroom through the only open door.

"What about Stella?" I said.

"Observant, aren't you. She has a room of her own. Sort of."

"I don't understand."

"There's a sleeping porch off my bedroom. She's well looked after. You'll see everyone's room eventually." She started down the stairs without letting me into any of the rooms.

We found the others outside. Without sitting down, Dottie explained the routine. "We rotate who prepares dinner and cleans up the dishes. We're in charge of our own breakfasts and lunches. Won't matter to you after tonight. You've got your own kitchen in the cottage." She made clear that Richard and I were the hired help.

When we finished clearing, Dottie told us we'd play charades. She dictated the game and the teams. Dottie, me,

Thick Thelma, and Lucy in the Sky on one team. Richard, Skinny Stella, Plain Jane, and Barb the Bard on the other. Jane winked at me and mouthed, "House mother."

We went onto the front porch where we were safely screened from mosquitoes that would appear with the setting sun. The porch had an eastern exposure for the sunrise. It extended the length of the house and had a wonderful view of Lake Winnipesaukee. A table at one end held a puzzle, half completed. The box showed an image of The Old Man in the Mountain. Six small end tables were scattered throughout the porch. I noticed a volume of Mary Oliver's poetry on one, a half-knit scarf on another. It looked like each of the women had an assigned table. They had figured out how to live together and separately with Dottie clearly in charge. I wondered if there was any other kind of hierarchy. Where were the intimacies? The rivalries? I'd find out soon enough.

We cleared an area in the center of the porch and lined up mesh chairs so our teams faced each other. We were two chairs short. Dottie commanded Richard, "Go into the dining room and get us two more chairs."

Richard glanced at me, his expression showing the impatience I knew he was feeling. Catering to old people wasn't one of his strengths and I'd had to convince him that this job was the only way to rebuild our finances. When he returned with ladder back chairs, I silently congratulated the women for attaching cushions to them. They'd ease the stress on their lower backs. We took our sides and each came up with a phrase for the opposite team. Eight charades before Richard and I could go back to our cottage and each other.

As soon as Lucy in the Sky started acting out her phrase, I knew I could abbreviate her name to Diamond Lucy. Her rings flashed through her gesticulations. Her hands signaled seven words; two fingers, second word; fingers placed on her arm, two syllables. She pointed to her ring and Dottie called out "diamond." Thick Thelma followed with "diamonds are forever."

"Seven words, Thelma," Dottie chastised.

Lucy signaled word number four. She circled her arms over her head. My team called out "large," "full," "balloon." Lucy shook her head no at all our guesses and went to the first word. Little word. Thelma called out words that weren't small, "together," "finger," "diamond," though we already had that word. I cut her off with "A."

Lucy nodded "yes" and signaled word number six, another small word that Dottie got with "the." She went back to the fourth word, this time drawing a small square in the air, erasing it, and drawing a bigger square. I called out, "Big," "A Diamond as Big as the Ritz" just as the timer buzzed. I suspected that Richard contributed that title. He loved Fitzgerald.

"Not fair," said Lucy. "You have to choose things we all know. I never heard of 'A Diamond as Big as the Ritz.'"

Barb the Bard explained. "It's a short story. By Fitzgerald. It popped into my head when you were inspecting your nails. Polish holding up?"

I was wrong about Richard's choice. I could remember

Barb by her first name alone. Her words were barbs aimed at Lucy. There was tension, if not outright hostility, between them.

As we continued playing, I formed opinions. Richard would say I was too quick to judge. But these weren't judgments, they were observations, fluid and evolving.

The tension between Lucy and Barb increased rather than decreased. Stella was the least robust, skinny, stooped, and losing lung capacity because of her scoliosis. She'd nearly fallen when she acted out the "down" of "Down by the Riverside." I'd chosen the charade, forgetting that these were old women who might have trouble bending over. At least I'd stopped myself from offering *The Hunchback of Notre Dame.*

Thelma's response to a seven-word clue with a three-word answer characterized her guesses throughout the evening. Quick, but often nonsensical. I understood Dottie's guess of "digging a hole" for "planting a garden," but Thelma's guess of "flying a plane" was as off as her continued miscounting of words in the clues.

Jane turned out to be anything but plain. Her acting out of "Send in the Clowns" was hilarious. She went from mimicking clown make-up to imitating a crowd of clowns coming out of a tiny car. She was as agile as Stella was stiff.

After Richard and I said goodnight, we walked to the edge of the dock before we went back to our cottage. We took off our shoes and dangled our feet in the lake. I took his hand and said, "It's beautiful here."

"Those old ladies aren't beautiful. I don't know if I can do it."

"Please try. We need this job. There'll be enough work to keep you busy, more than the nursing I'll have to do. You can find reasons to go to the mainland most days."

"Where I don't know anyone. They won't even let me cook. That's what I'm good at."

"You can cook for us."

He stood up and pulled me to him. "I'll try. It is beautiful on a night like this." He wrapped his arms around me and whispered, "Let's go christen that cottage bed."

His kiss made me think that we'd be okay.

By the time August arrived, Richard and I had established a routine. While I checked on the women, he'd continue with whatever project Dottie had assigned him or take the boat for the fifteen-minute ride to Wolfeboro for supplies. He'd repaired windows, rebuilt a shed, cleared debris from under the front porch. A week ago he started to stain the shingles. Their dark brown was turning darker.

The house would have felt sinister except for the island's beauty. We'd explored every corner of its ten acres. The sandy beach where the women swam, the stand of pine trees on one end of the island where herons were nesting, the boulder shadowed by oaks and maples that Dottie had marked as a graveyard. Most of the island was rocky but here the soil was rich enough to coax ferns to grow. We broke all the environmental rules by feeding the mallards that gathered on the rocky shore next to the dock. No one came to check. We were an island unto ourselves.

I'd learned that none of my six charges had ever fit the dreaded word "spinster." They'd all been married and widowed. I couldn't think of them as patients because they were remarkably robust. Dottie took nothing except an occasional ibuprofen. Lucy had diabetes that I needed to monitor, but she refused to give up her evening glass of wine despite my cautions to her. Barb took amiodarone for heart arrhythmia and Jane took fludrocortisone for hypotension. I gave them pills morning and evening even though they could remember them without me. It made me feel useful.

I'd done a quick assessment of Thelma and knew that she was descending into some form of dementia, likely Alzheimer's. I took away her pill box when I saw that she'd either forget a day or would take two or three days' worth of pills at once. They weren't dangerous. A daily vitamin, calcium for her bones, ibuprofen for her arthritis. I made her an appointment with Doctor Savage and would suggest that he prescribe some kind of cholinesterase inhibitor. It wouldn't stop Alzheimer's, but it might manage any behavioral symptoms. I could monitor side effects— nausea, diarrhea, weight loss, fatigue. In the meantime, I made sure that her silver hair was combed and the outfit she chose for the day was appropriate for the weather. She could still follow the exercises on the DVD they played.

It didn't take long for me to learn that my charges wanted a companion more than a nurse, a confidante to hear their grievances with each other. And their confessions. Bit by bit, they hinted at secrets they'd been holding onto for more years than I'd been alive.

In late August, Stella became the first to reveal more details about her life. As frail as she looked, she had a strong heart and perfect blood pressure, but the yearly shots she got for osteoporosis weren't enough to stop the ravages of her bent spine. I managed to start her on some breathing exercises to build her lung capacity.

She told me about herself one morning when I went to her room to massage her back. The massages helped her to get moving in the morning and I'd taken to giving her one every couple of days. She spoke in a voice as strong as her body was thin. "We're not just a bunch of old ladies forced to live together because we don't have families. I have a daughter. Cynthia. You remind me of her. Not now, of course. She's sixty-eight, but she's still straight and strong. Her hair's gray, but it's cut like yours. And she has wrinkles. Lots of them. Too much time in the sun."

"Where is she now?"

"I don't know."

I pulled up her cotton nightgown and helped her get her arms out of the sleeves so I could massage her back. I pressed gently along her lats and her rhomboids and dorsal muscles. Even if I dared to press hard enough to release the knots I felt, I didn't have a good angle. My touch was gentle, just enough to get her blood flowing. "That must be hard."

"I'm used to it. She's off again with that husband of hers.

Galloping around the world. Go look at the postcards on my dresser." She turned over, put her arms back into her sleeves, and sat up, signaling that the massage was over.

I went to her dresser and looked through postcards scattered among a half-dozen framed photos of her daughter. Gamla Stan in Stockholm, medieval buildings in Maastricht, Netherlands, a winery in France. Then a shift to Asia, Singapore, Vietnam, and a fancy hotel called The Empire in Brunei, a country I'd never heard of. All had brief notes on the back, written in a careful hand and signed "Love always."

"You must miss her."

"Not so much. I gave them the money so they wouldn't hang around like martyrs making me feel like a burden."

"That's generous," I said, hoping to learn more about where her money came from.

"Can't line my coffin with money." She got off the bed and nudged me away from her dresser so she could get her clothes. "My husband left me plenty. That's about all he was good for."

I wanted to hear more of her story. "Did you meet him at UNH?"

"He was a Dartmouth man. Never let me forget it. We met on a blind date when he came to UNH with the man Jane married. Jane's husband was a good man and a good father. Arty—that was my husband—wasn't much of a father. He traveled a lot. That's how Cynthia caught the bug." She arranged a pair of slip-on pants, a T-shirt, and a sweatshirt on the bed. "Arty was an international sales rep for Coca Cola. At first we lived in Atlanta where Coke is headquartered. Once he started to travel, we were able to move back to New Hampshire. Nashua, close to the airport in Boston. The romance went out of our marriage when that happened. He traveled too much, probably had a few affairs with exotic women. He never said and I never asked. Once Cynthia started school, Arty left me alone to do what I wanted."

"What was that? What did you want?"

"Not a lot of professions for women in those days. Nurse or teacher. Not like the choices you young women have."

"I chose nursing. I like it."

"You're good at it. I'm glad you're here. If I'd had more choice I might have been a researcher, found a vaccine the way those folks found one for Covid. Not a path I could find living in Nashua, so I chose teaching. Turns out I liked it. Liked teaching those kids that you get sick from germs, not from cold weather."

"Did they believe you?"

"Sometimes they'd argue. 'My mother told me.' That kind of thing."

"What about Cynthia and her husband?"

"Researchers, both of them. Plant genetics. I don't approve of all this manipulation of nature." She took a towel from the towel rack that was identical to the ones in all the rooms and picked up the carrier for her toiletries from the dresser. "My turn in the bathroom. Dottie manages our schedule."

She left me alone in her room, feeling that if her life had

been thwarted, it hadn't been empty. Dottie was wrong. Stella might be skinny and stooped, but if her body could easily be pushed over, her spirit couldn't be.

I glanced around the room that was color-coded in the yellow that Dottie had chosen for Stella's comforter and the towels she had carried to the bathroom. The room had been a sleeping porch, small but with windows on three sides. In this summer weather, it felt as if she were sleeping outside. She had to go through Dottie's room to get anywhere in the house. If Dottie wasn't out of bed when I came to give Stella a massage, she'd be sitting, regal against the purple she'd assigned herself.

I inhaled a good breath of air from the open window. It cleared away the anxiety that had been mounting during the month I'd gotten to know these women and the resentments that lay beneath the surface of their friendships.

I arranged six chairs and six mats next to them so everyone could see the television in what Dottie called the exercise room. Watching these women move through their exercise program had become one of my jobs. I took a disc out of a case whose cover was designed with three interwoven M's, the logo for Mindful Movement with Meredith. There were two discs, three programs on each. The bio on the back of the case identified Meredith as a fitness instructor with multiple degrees and her own studio in Boston. Her photo showed a tall, thin woman dressed in Lycra. She stood on one leg next to a chair, the other bent and lifted a foot off the floor. A thin booklet inside the case showed her in other positions for other DVD sets. In one she posed on the floor, legs in a V position in the air, arms touching her toes. I was small and agile, but I couldn't get into a position like that.

Meredith knew how to market herself. I cringed at her self-promotion, but I had to admit that she was good. She led the elderly through six half-hour sessions, a seventh day for rest. Each session started with breath work and stretches and ended with stretches and breath work in reverse order. With Meredith's instructions and my help, Stella's lungs were improving.

The second half of each day's program emphasized one exercise—arm strength, leg strength, flexibility, cardio, stretching, balance. Tuesday was for balance. Only Barb didn't need a chair to stabilize her. She told me she concentrated by reciting poems she'd memorized. Thelma had the hardest time, so I made sure to stand behind her in case she fell. The session ended with Meredith saying, "No worries. If this wasn't your best day, the next one might be. Keep on moving mindfully."

Dottie took over when Meredith finished. She turned off the DVD player and faced the others, dictating, not negotiating. "Tomorrow's Wednesday. We'll do the arm strength program early. We're going on the *Mount Washington* for the 11:30 boat trip around Winnipesaukee."

Everyone nodded then rolled their mats and got off the floor in the way Meredith taught them. Stella pushed herself up and held onto her chair, standing as straight as her bent spine would allow. She announced, "I'm not going."

Dottie cinched her mat with a yoga strap. "Of course you are. The tickets are all paid for."

"I've been on that boat ride a million times. I'm not going."

"Don't exaggerate. I reserved six tickets."

"Nataki can go. You're not the boss of me. Besides, most of the money in our house account came from me." She positioned her mat under her arm and left the room.

Dottie recovered her composure and said to me, "You'll go then. It will be a better trip without Stella. Tell that husband of yours that he needs to fix the screen I showed him. He should have done it yesterday."

"He had to buy the screening in Wolfeboro yesterday. He got back late."

Tension had been building between Dottie and Richard ever since we arrived. He called her Queen of the Crotchety Cult. I was starting to think he was right. We were only a month into our experiment in island living. We needed it to work out. Besides, I liked these women who tried his patience. Caregiving was my strength, not his.

The *Mount Washington* was filled with passengers who had boarded at its Weirs Beach home port. We waited in a short line to join them, earning a few glances from young couples who looked like honeymooners and parents with young children who stared at five old ladies who looked like their great-grandmothers. I couldn't blame them. Thelma's hat made her look like Minnie Pearl. One smart-aleck boy nodded and said "How-dee." He must have liked old-time country music.

We all wore sun hats and had lathered on sunscreen against the August heat. I thought of Stella's comment about her daughter. "Too much time in the sun." Two teenage girls brushed past as if we were pariahs. I felt protective and wanted to tell the girls that they'd one day lose their muscled arms and thin waists and glowing hair. Their smooth faces would bare the myriad wrinkles of lives long lived. If they were lucky.

We found our way to the back deck and a vacant table. As the boat pulled away from the Wolfeboro town dock, I waved to Richard, wondering what he'd do for the day. He left the island as much as he could, escaped what he called mindless chores and the chit-chat of old women. Maybe he'd go back, appreciate its quiet and cool off from the heat and humidity of midday by swimming. Stella wouldn't bother him. Instead, he walked past Dottie's boat toward the town center.

I found the side deck and listened to tourists talk about iconic spots they planned to visit in the White Mountains of New Hampshire. Mount Washington's Cog Railway, the Flume, the Kancamagus Highway. I'd been to them all as a child and still remembered the tight boulders that formed the Orange Crush and the Lemon Squeeze in the Polar Caves. New Hampshire lived off the tourist economy made possible by thousands of workers who couldn't afford to live along the shores of Lake Winnipesaukee. The taxes on even small homes that had been handed down through generations would be more than what Richard and I had paid for rent on our Boston apartment when we were both employed in the city. I wondered how Dottie managed. Was she living off the money the others brought to their experiment in communal living?

I walked to the back deck again. Barb and Jane were standing at the rail. Jane turned to me and winked. "We're looking for the Loch Dot monster." Her smile told me she was joking but I could tell that I wasn't the only one who knew that Dottie could be a bossy house mother.

Jane turned back to face the lake. She put her hands to her ears, ignoring the taped voice telling us that the original *Mount Washington* had been a paddle boat carrying mail and passengers in 1872. Dottie and Lucy were playing Scrabble, ignoring both the factual information and the scenery. Thelma faced the back of the boat, mesmerized by the piped-in voice touting Wolfeboro as the oldest resort area in the United States. I watched the shoreline recede and thought about how Wolfeboro wore its quaintness like a badge.

I left my oversized travel bag that served as an emergency medical kit on the table and wandered to the front deck. The chairs were all taken, but only a few people stood along the railing. If Richard had been with me, we could have played the scene from *Titanic* where Jack holds onto Rose as she hangs over the front bow and says, "I'm flying." Except this was Winnipesaukee and a disembodied voice was telling me that the lake was twenty-one miles long, nine miles wide, and a hundred and eighty feet deep at its lowest depth. A sixty-three mile road surrounded the island. I'd convince Richard that we need to take a day off, rent a car, and drive around the lake. Escape Heron Island and his impatience with the aged.

The loudspeaker turned off so I could concentrate on the scenery. The lake was beautiful, but not as beautiful as it must have been when only the Abenaki lived along a shore barren of houses. They would have fished in water free of the boats that now sailed or pulled water skiers or showed off the power of their motors, their drivers pushing against the forty-five mile per hour speed limit. Whether Richard or I drove the boat, Dottie always reminded us of that limit.

I smelled her before she appeared next to me. Dottie. The sunscreen she wore was laced with coconut. "I've been summering on Heron Island for sixty-eight years and this is the first time I've been on the *Mount Washington*."

"Really? I would have thought you'd take guests on the boat every season."

"Guests always went. Charles would buy their tickets and let us have a few hours to ourselves. Thelma, Barb, Lucy, Jane. They've all been on the cruise."

"And Stella?"

"You heard her. Not a million times, but she went during those summers like everyone else. Don't get me wrong. She's a good friend and I rely on her."

I wondered if she meant for her money. "How does it feel being on this boat for the first time?"

"A little disappointing. Too many people. Too much chatter. The information coming over the loudspeaker is annoying. It sounds like some space alien talking through an electrical storm."

I smiled at the image. Two boats ahead of us were racing each other, spewing noise and enormous wakes behind them.

Dottie yelled at them. "Slow down, you assholes."

"Good choice of word," I said. "It must have been quieter when you first started coming here."

"It was. Charles and I had a good run."

"Want to tell me about him?" I used the opening to try to learn more about Dottie's background the way I had learned about Stella's.

"He was a priest."

I felt a heavy skip in my heart. "A priest?"

"Don't be shocked. He left the priesthood before we married. He led our P.F. group."

"P.F.?"

"Pilgrim Fellowship. That's what he called the group. Catholic kids couldn't go to the one with the Congregational kids, so he started one for us. Stole the name. He grew up Congregational. When he went to Boston College, he converted, but he was nostalgic for his P.F. days. He could have risen in the priesthood. I put a stop to that." She took her hat off and rotated it by the rim. "This is the last gift he gave me. Fifteen summers ago, a few months before he died. Of a heart attack, so you don't need to ask. He was ninety-two, just like I am now."

I risked a question. "How did it happen that you married a priest?"

"I got pregnant."

"Pregnant?"

"Don't be shocked."

We were echoes, repeating each other's words.

Dottie began explaining before I could ask another question. "Priests have needs, too. It happened right after I graduated from college. I was twenty-one and he was thirty-six. Consenting adults. Isn't that what they call it today?" She put her hat on, adjusting it so no sun fell on the face she'd managed to keep smooth and free of damage. "One of the bishops offered to help me find a place to deliver the baby into the adoption system. Or to have an abortion if I chose that."

Now I was shocked, though I shouldn't be. This was a church that relocated pedophile priests so they could continue abusing altar boys. Its preaching on the right-to-life stopped when it was inconvenient. "You did neither," I managed to say.

"Charles wouldn't hear of it. He had to go through a process called laicization to get divorced from his vows. They moved it along fast enough for us to get married before Jonathan was born and Charles took over his family business."

I wanted to ask why she still listened to Father Eddy's Catholic Mass on Sundays, but decided on something more neutral. "What was the business?"

"A sawmill in Lincoln. He sold it in 1995. Gave us

plenty of money to both retire. Running a bit low now."

"Both? Did you also have a job?"

"Don't underestimate us. We may be old women, but we all have college degrees. I was a math major. When the kids were old enough I took over the accounting for the mill."

"Kids?" I wasn't sure how many more questions she'd answer.

"Jonathan and James. Jonathan Edwards, the Puritan minister and James Edwards after James II, the last Catholic English king. We found it amusing to play with the names."

"Where are they now?"

"You are a bundle of questions, aren't you. It's not a secret. James is doing missionary work in Papua New Guinea. Jonathan died."

"I'm so sorry."

The recorded voice intruded on what she'd been about to say. It explained that we were now in the part of the lake called The Broads, named because it was a broad expanse of water that contained none of the 264 islands that dotted the lake. Dottie reached for my hand as the voice explained how after the first glaciation period the lake flowed southeast then changed course in the second glaciation period. The voice summed up, "It now flows west to the Pemigewasset and together they form the Merrimack. A bit of Winnipesaukee accompanied Henry David Thoreau in 1849 on his trip down the Merrimack and Concord Rivers."

Dottie ignored the information dump and grasped my hand that was holding onto the railing. Her blue veins pulsed. "He died out here on The Broads. We had a sailboat then and he got caught in a storm. The lake can get violent fast. We found the boat capsized. He was trapped beneath it. We buried his ashes in a grove of trees behind the house. Charles is there, too. Our little Heron Island graveyard."

"I know. Richard and I often walk there."

She continued in the staccato voice that sounded like a wall she'd built against her feelings. "One son dead at twenty. The other lost to me in whatever missionary outpost he goes to. Now I listen to Father Eddy on Sundays and wonder why I cling to a Catholic ritual. I lost my faith when I had sex with a priest, but the ritual brings me comfort."

She pulled her hand away to signal that she'd finished her story. I watched her disappear around the side of the boat, her back hunched with the memory of her grief.

Richard was waiting for us at the dock, talking with someone who looked familiar. As we descended the ramp, I had to grab Thelma, who headed toward town instead of our Heron Island boat.

Richard greeted me with a hug. The others gathered around the woman he was with. We all recognized her. "You're Meredith of Mindful Movement," I said.

"I am. Richard tells me you and your friends"—she nodded toward them—"exercise every day to my elderly program."

"Senior program," said Dottie. "Elderly's for the senile."

"From what Richard tells me, you'll never be elderly." She spoke in the same accentless voice she'd cultivated for her films. Without make-up and expensive Lycra, she looked ordinary, sporty instead of choreographed.

Thelma lifted her arms and rotated them in a circle the way Mindful Movement instructed. Meredith reached for her arm and felt her muscle. "Nicely toned. I'll bet you're a swimmer."

She was being diplomatic. Thelma's arms had three inches of flab surrounding what was left of her muscles. But she was right. Thelma went into the lake every day. I always made sure I was there to watch what passed for swimming.

Dottie looked from Meredith to Richard. "Has Nataki's husband been showing you around Wolfeboro while we were hearing a canned lecture about the history of Lake Winnipesaukee?"

Richard ignored the innuendo in Dottie's reference to him as my husband. "I recognized her when I stopped at the Burnt Timber for a beer and a burger. Don't worry, Dottie, I just had one beer. No drunk boat driving."

Meredith watched more people getting off the *Mount Washington*. "Too much of that on this lake. Someone dies on it every year because of drinking."

Dottie said nothing, just turned away to look out at the lake.

"That's why we don't let Barb drive the boat," said Lucy, who'd been complaining all month that Barb's nightly glass of wine had turned to half a bottle. Once a week, Richard carried a case of wine for all of us to share on the island. He justified his purchase with the twenty percent off for a case at the New Hampshire Liquor and Wine Outlet.

Meredith waved at a man who looked as fit as she was and a little girl who was holding his hand. "There are my folks now. It was nice meeting you all. Thanks for the tour, Richard. No worries." She ended our meeting the way she ended each of her exercise sessions.

Richard watched her as she walked away. I wondered how long ago he'd had that beer. No worries, indeed, I hoped.

"I know what this means." Thelma's voice was as bright as her silver hair that shone in the September light. Her mood didn't match her diagnosis, but she seemed less confused until we got to the boat. "Why isn't Howard driving?" More and more she mistook Richard for her husband. She could still find her way around the house, but we monitored her in the kitchen. Despite the cooler days of fall, she still swam in the afternoon, but never alone.

I opened my purse to find the keys to the boat. They were hidden under a bag from the pharmacy with the donepezil Doctor Savage had prescribed to help Thelma's memory as she descended deeper into Alzheimer's.

"You know what this means?" I repeated Thelma's words to see if she had processed the diagnosis. Doctor

Savage had spoken directly to her, treating her with dignity as he explained how she could manage the disease. "Mrs. Johnson, don't be afraid to ask all those friends you live with for help. I know Nataki from when I was helping out at the hospital in Boston. She'll take good care of you."

"Tanaki?" She'd looked away from Doctor Savage to me and said, "Alice, who's that?" She often talked to me as if I were her sister.

She stepped into the boat without needing help and settled into the seat. I untied the ropes from the mooring and got in beside her. She took hold of my hand to stop me from turning on the ignition. "Don't start it yet. I know Howard's dead. You're Nataki. Our nurse. Dottie, Stella, Barb, Lucy, Jane. We're in the little old age home we laughed about when we were all young. Now we call it the last exit."

I wondered how long she'd have moments of lucidity like this. "Right. On Heron Island. We need to go back there now. Richard and I are taking the night off. Having dinner in Wolfeboro."

"You can give me five minutes," she snapped, hostile in a way I'd not heard before.

I left the key in the ignition and rotated so I could look at her. The position was uncomfortable, so I lifted my legs onto the seat. With my knees bent, I leaned against the side of the boat to look straight at her. "Do you want to talk about it?"

"It?" She kept her eyes focused on the dock where a family with three kids were all eating ice cream cones.

"Alzheimer's. You know what Doctor Savage told you."

"Of course I do. I'm not senile."

Yet, I thought.

"I used to love ice cream," she said. "Howard and I used to go to Grant's Café at UNH for it. That nice train station they turned into an ice cream stand wasn't there in the old days, but the ice cream at Grant's was good. I always got chocolate and Howard got vanilla. He was a vanilla kind of guy. Tasteful, not too dramatic. Except that one time."

"That one time? You want to tell me about it?"

"We kept it a secret. Never even talked about it together all the years we were married. It was a terrible crime. I think our punishment was not being able to have children."

"I'm listening." I tried to imagine how ice cream could involve a terrible crime.

"We broke in. Took ice cream out of the freezer and left it on the counter of the soda fountain. Pistachio. Not our usual. It was St. Patrick's Day."

"That's not much of a crime."

"There's more. Howard proposed while we were scooping out ice cream cones. We broke into the cash register and stole all the money. For our honeymoon. It wasn't much, not quite fifty dollars. We'd have been okay if we hadn't turned on the jukebox and started to dance."

"You got caught?"

"Almost. A policeman heard us. Howard picked up one of those huge buckets of ice cream and hit him on the back of the head. Knocked him out."

"How badly did he hurt him?"

"Him?" She was drifting, losing track of the story she'd been telling.

"The policeman Howard hit with the ice cream container."

"Look at those kids. They shouldn't eat ice cream. It's bad for you. I never eat it myself."

She was right. I'd never seen her with ice cream. Whatever the end of the story was, I wouldn't find it out today. I took my legs off the seat, turned on the ignition, and backed the boat away from its mooring.

Thelma stayed quiet on the way back to the island. When we docked, the iridescent green of the mallard swimming along the shore made me think of Thelma's pistachio ice cream. Whatever she was thinking as I walked her to her room stayed locked in her mind until we reached her door and she pointed to the caricature. "Lucy drew this, drew one for all of us."

"They're wonderful." Lucy had captured everyone's personality. Her drawing of Thelma was calm, almost ghostly in its muted tones. She even managed to find a silver paint to capture the color of Thelma's hair.

Thelma opened her door and picked up a book from her nightstand. *And Then There Were None.* "I can still follow an Agatha Christie mystery." She settled herself onto the bed, laying the book unopened beside her.

The afternoon sun shone on her bed, bathing her in a circle where she'd be able to read or sleep. Her room was like everyone's. A single bed, a dressing table with enough drawers for clothes, a small closet. A silvery gray comforter on the bed and matching towels on the towel rack. A bland room with only one photo of her husband on her dressing table to personalize it. It was as if she were burying the guilt that had haunted her. I left her to whatever memories she could conjure and found the others at the picnic table in the back yard.

"Well?" Dottie spoke first. "What did he say?"

"What we all know. Thelma has Alzheimer's. He gave her a prescription. It won't stop it, but it might help slow the progression of memory loss."

"And turn her into a zombie," said Jane. "I watched my mother die of Alzheimer's. They called it senility back then. I'm glad you're here so we won't have to change her diapers."

"That won't happen for a while. Just be patient with her. Treat her like normal."

"Did Doctor Savage tell her?" Lucy was twisting the diamond on her left hand. The polish on her fingernails needed redoing. Unusual. Something seemed to have been troubling her all week.

"He did. She was lucid for a bit, drifting into a memory of Howard and UNH and an episode in some place where they used to buy ice cream."

"Grant's Café," said Stella. "Arty and I used to go there every Friday. Until someone broke in the end of our senior year."

Jane stood up from the bench where she had lost the sun. She walked to a spot where it was still shining. "They left ice cream melting on the counter, stole money out of the cash register, and knocked out a policeman. Barb should write a poem about it. Attack of the waffle cone."

"It's not funny," said Lucy. "I knew him." She also moved away from the table to stand next to Jane.

Barb shot an innuendo at Lucy. "More than knew him."

"Doesn't matter. He died." She walked away from us and went toward the side of the house.

I clenched my teeth to keep from bursting out with Thelma's confession.

"Don't listen to her," said Barb. "Whoever broke in didn't kill him. He died just a few years ago in a skiing accident. Lucy can tell you the story. I've always wondered if the two of them broke into Grant's."

"That's enough." Dottie stopped the conversation. "It was a long time ago. Let the past be the past."

I left them to their memories of a time I no longer thought was simple. Whatever happened at that café, Thelma had married Howard and was fixating now on ice cream that she never ate. Maybe she'd heard too many jokes about someone named Howard Johnson.

Richard stopped the boat in front of a cottage cradled among several granite boulders. Its dock sat in water that was deep and clear and glacial. He got out of the boat and reached down to pull me beside him.

"What are we doing here? Aren't we going to the Wolfeboro Inn?" It was my twenty-fifth birthday and he'd promised me a dinner out.

"Help me tie up the boat and I'll show you."

I wondered if he had rented the cottage for the night, if he was going to make me the kind of elegant meal he used to prepare when he was a chef.

He said nothing, just held onto my hand and led me to a white cottage that must have been one of the oldest on Lake Winnipesaukee. He unlocked the door and we stepped inside. The walls and floors were knotty pine, stained in a light color and polished to a high sheen. A wall of windows facing the lake kept it from being dark. I could see that the wall had been renovated. One of the windows was shaped like a door that must have once opened onto a porch that was no longer there. A porch would have blocked the light that was now shining into the open concept living space.

I studied it, trying to figure out why Richard had brought me here. It wasn't to make a romantic dinner. The dining room table was pine like the rest of the room, but there was no table setting or candles or flowers. Two sofas were pushed together back to back. One faced the lake, the other a fireplace framed by granite rocks and a line of bookcases.

I looked at the lone photo on a bookcase that held enough books to keep people well-read through a long summer season. The photo showed three people on the dock, smiling, the lake sparkling behind them. A man and a little girl and a woman all too familiar despite wearing a bathing suit designed for swimming instead of Lycra pants and a tank top designed with a three M logo.

I found enough breath to say, "Meredith."

"I need to get away from the island. Those old women are destroying me. I don't want them to destroy our marriage." He touched the scar on his temple the way he sometimes did when he was nervous.

I knew he was as stressed on Heron Island as he'd been in Boston when we were shut up during the pandemic. "Get away from them or from me?"

"Them. I started going to the Burnt Timber on Fridays. It turned out that's when Meredith would drop her husband off and take their daughter to swim lessons. Mark's a basketball coach at B.U. Once the season starts, they won't be able to get here often. They need a caretaker for the winter. I said I'd stay here."

"What about your other caretaking job? What about me?"

"I've thought it all through. After I leave Dottie's boat at Goodhue's for the winter, I'll use Mark's. When the lake starts to freeze, I'll stay on the island until it's solid enough for the snowmobile. It won't take long. Eventually I'll be able to drive Mark's jeep on it. I'll do the job but I can't spend twenty-four hours a day with six old ladies."

"I like them."

"I know you do. This will work. You can stay here some nights. I'll spend some nights on the island. Maybe you'll even get your parents to visit." He was being conciliatory. He knew my parents had rented their house in Cambridge and were in Edinburgh where my father was on a faculty exchange teaching anthropology. Calls on Skype were keeping us connected.

I looked again at the photo of three smiling faces and imagined that kind of family for us. "What happens in the summer when this family comes back?"

"We'll figure something out. Maybe my new job will turn into something more permanent."

"Your new job? What are you talking about? You said you'll still be caretaker."

"I need to work in a kitchen. A stove and a couple of pots in the cottage aren't enough. I found a job at the Wolfeboro Inn. Just for Sunday brunch. Let's go. Dinner tonight is on them."

He held my hand and led me to the door. He released it to lock the cottage. I could see Heron Island bathed in a blood red sunset. Was it setting on our marriage that was under too much stress? Richard answered my unspoken question with the kind of kiss that had gone out of our lives since we'd been living on the island.

"At least we're not bobbing for apples." Richard sliced a triangle eye in the pumpkin he was carving. He'd agreed to join our Halloween party, then he'd take the boat to Goodhue's to store it for the winter. Our arrangement wasn't ideal, but it was working. Dottie was happy that Richard had been able to use the boat to bring enough firewood to the island for the winter. He'd put up the storm windows, drained the outdoor pipes, covered over the garden, and done everything else she'd asked.

"Wait until you see the costumes I've outfitted them

in," I said as I carved a tiny scar like Richard's next to my pumpkin's eye.

"Did they do all this last Halloween? I can't imagine how they've been managing. There was a ton of work getting this place ready for winter." He finished his pumpkin, stuck a candle into it, and set it on the dock next to seven other jack-o'-lanterns. The faces ranged from clown-like to ghost-like to bemused. The grin on my pumpkin and the hint of a scar next to the eye looked sinister.

"They managed the way they're doing now. With a caretaker who came out every week." I tried to keep the note of resentment out of my voice.

"I'm happier this way. It's better for us."

He could last for years with this arrangement, but I couldn't. I was starting to adopt the mannerisms of even active old people, rocking in a chair and staring at the lake, napping in the afternoon, checking the time to see how long before dinner. Not that dinner mattered. I mostly ate alone in the cottage whenever I felt hungry.

I wrapped the pumpkin seeds in the newspaper Richard had piled them on. "Time for our costumes. I promised them. It'll be fun."

Without agreeing, he followed me to the compost pile he'd created by making a hole inside a square of four hay bales, a trick from his days growing up on a farm. If the compost wasn't ready by spring planting time, the hay bales would be rotted enough for mulch. We'd keep turning over the compost, buy new bales and start another pile.

Richard found the pitchfork and turned the pumpkin seeds into the pile of vegetable scraps. "One spring planting only, then we should quit. If you want to be a geriatric nurse, you can be one off-island."

"I like my job. Besides, Heron Island's perfect for gardening. No woodchucks or skunks or deer to enjoy a garden salad." I took the pitchfork from him and held it between us. "*American Gothic.* I should have thought of that for our costumes."

"What will I be? Peter Rabbit? Mr. McGregor? The Great Pumpkin?"

"Follow me and you'll see."

We walked past the house to get to our cottage. Despite the closed windows I could smell the chili that Jane and Barb had made. Richard wouldn't like it. Too tomato-y. Too bland. Not enough beans. It didn't matter. He could make something else when he got back to Wolfeboro.

Inside the cottage, I stopped him from going into the spare bedroom where I'd laid out the costumes on the bed. "Not yet." I led him into the bedroom we shared and unzipped his jacket. I helped him take it off, then ran my hands along the image of Mount Washington on his light-weight hoodie. He pulled it over his head. We copied moves—shirts, shoes and socks, pants, underwear—and fell onto the bed.

An hour and a half later, Richard and I stood in the living room, hurriedly dressed in unimaginative costumes. Each of my costumed ninety-year-olds would make a grand entrance from the less than grand staircase. It had been built against the living room wall, a banister serving in place of another wall. Uncarpeted and dangerous if anyone forgot to hold on to the banister. Richard would have to guess who or what they were dressed as. When they were all assembled, I'd join them and Richard would take our photo. He told me it was a stupid idea, but I said it would be amusing.

Barb was the first to come down. I couldn't hide the map of wrinkles on her face, but I'd fashioned what little hair she had so it was pulled severely back from her face. Gray instead of dark, but the effect worked because she held her glasses in her hand as if they were a pen. She wore a black dress scooped at the neck. A black ribbon edged in white fell like a necklace, crossed and held together with a gold pin.

"Some old lady," said Richard.

"We're all old. Because we cannot stop for death." Barb paraphrased an Emily Dickinson poem.

"Emily Dickinson." Richard surprised me until I remembered that someone had read Dickinson's poem at his mother's funeral and I read it a year later when his father died from Covid and we'd been the only two at the gravesite.

I thought of his loss of family as I watched Thelma, widowed and childless, descend the stairs. She was dressed as a pumpkin in an orange jumpsuit stuffed with a pillow to make her pudgy waist even pudgier. At the bottom of the stairs, she took off the green ribbon I'd fastened in her hair to represent the pumpkin's stem. She began twisting it with her fingers, her face more vacant than the ones we'd carved into our real pumpkins.

Richard dutifully guessed Linus's Great Pumpkin and waited for the next appearance. One by one, each person descended the stairs. Stella as Little Red Riding Hood, hunched under a hooded cape fashioned out of an old bathrobe. Plain Jane in the knee-length, white skirt and navy blue sweater she'd worn as a UNH Pepcat. She still carried herself with the enthusiasm of a cheerleader.

Lucy wore a blue nightgown cinched at the waist and a white hat trimmed in orange. She carried a bouquet of dried flowers as the final touch of Renoir's painting *Woman in a Blue Dress*. In the last four months, I'd come to admire the knowledge of paintings she'd acquired as an art major. Often I'd see her with an easel set up somewhere on the island. Because her hands shook when she painted, the watercolors bled into interesting patterns.

Dottie made a grand last entrance. She wore her wedding dress, one that had been loose around the waist to disguise her pregnancy. Once defiantly white, it was now yellowed with age. A piece of netting laced with dead flowers served as a veil. Richard recognized her costume immediately. "Miss Havisham. *Great Expectations*. Where did you all get these costumes?"

Dottie raised her veil. "Nataki's been helping us ever since you moved off the island. Barb had the black dress, Lucy had a blue nightgown, Jane had her old cheerleading outfit, and I've had my wedding dress stored in a trunk ever since 1951. Lucy turned an old bathrobe into Stella's cape."

Thelma was trying to put the green ribbon back in her hair. I took it from her. "Let me help you." As I fastened it for her, I said, "We found this orange suit in Wolfeboro after one of her doctor appointments. Remember that day, Thelma?"

Thelma smiled and nodded. "Thank you." She was losing her mind but not her manners.

Barb brushed between Richard and me to get a camera from a table that held Halloween candy. "Let's get the photo over with." She gave it to Richard. "You any good with a real camera?"

I defended him. "He is."

Lucy stepped away from the group. "I'll arrange us."

"You would," said Barb, her voice carrying the tension that hadn't eased since that first day in July when Richard and I moved to the island.

"You, too. Get over there behind Stella." Lucy motioned me into the group and moved us into an arrangement. Stella in red in front of Barb in black. Dottie as Miss Havisham in the middle with Jane the cheerleader in front of her, her navy sweater accenting the yellowed white of Dottie's wedding gown. Thelma in orange was on the other side. Lucy positioned me in my blue nurse's scrubs next to Thelma then took her place behind the orange pumpkin.

"Okay, ladies, smile." Richard snapped one photo and held the camera to Lucy.

Lucy motioned him back. "Not yet. Take a few more." She directed us into a variety of positions. Chins raised in a glamor pose, arms folded in a pose of authority, fists raised in a cheer. When she was satisfied that Richard had taken enough pictures, she said, "Too bad Nataki didn't dress you as a daguerreotypist. Would have been better than that apron and chef's hat."

"I like it," said Dottie. "We should let him cook for us one of these days. Maybe at Thanksgiving. Hope you approve of our chili today, Richard. Time to eat."

We marched into the kitchen as if we were in a Halloween parade, filled our bowls, and carried them to the dining room table. This was one of the few times we'd eaten together since the hamburgers we had in July. My impressions of everyone had deepened more than changed. Barb the poet and Lucy the painter seemed like rivals, though I suspected there was more than an art competition behind the tension. Jane had the most energy and wit. Unlike her posture, Stella was emotionally sturdy. I still didn't know if Thelma had really been involved in the incident at Grant's, but her confusion was real and getting worse. Dottie was gruff and dictatorial, but I now knew that her manner allowed her to survive after the death of her son.

Richard commented that the chili was as good as Jesus and Angel's in Boston. It was the kind of quiet signal he tossed to me. He hated that restaurant and its fake Christian allusion. He stayed quiet through the rest of the meal. When he announced that it was time for him to leave and that he and I would light the pumpkins when we got to the dock, Jane got out of her chair and picked up her empty bowl. "We'll all go. A real parade. We should have seventy-six trombones." She put her fists to her mouth, pretending to play as she led the way in a marching gait.

Richard winked at me. He was more amused than I was. I wanted a last few minutes alone with him before he left for Wolfeboro. That didn't happen. We paraded from the kitchen, out the door to the dock. Each of us lit the candle in the pumpkin we'd carved. I steadied Thelma's hand so she wouldn't get the match too close to Dottie's wedding gown and set it on fire to burn like Miss Havisham's.

Richard gave me a quick kiss. Six pairs of hands applauded as we separated and he got into the boat. Eight pumpkins had eyes that lighted him on his way. I followed the others to the house to be sure that Thelma got her medicine. She was more confused than ever when I helped her out of her pumpkin costume and into pajamas and bed. I kissed her on the cheek as I said goodnight. She grabbed my hands, squeezed tighter than I thought possible and whispered, "You're good to me. So's Howard. I liked how the pumpkins shined on the water."

She confused names and jumped ideas, but she remembered the evening. I hoped for more months before she needed to be watched twenty-four seven. Every day she was retreating into the darkness of Alzheimer's. I locked her door with the latch Richard had improvised so she wouldn't wander in the night. Though she rarely woke, she had a call device if she needed anything.

I said goodnight to everyone and stopped at the dock to blow out the candles in the pumpkins. Thelma was right. The water was beautiful with their shining, still beautiful under the starlit sky when I blew them out.

I reached to the empty side of the bed for Richard. He'd returned from Wolfeboro when everyone had gone to bed so we could say what he called a proper goodnight. I'd watched him drive the boat away a second time under the light of the pumpkins.

I dressed hurriedly so I could check on Thelma before I fixed breakfast for myself. It was a cold morning and I could see the first skim of ice along the shore. It would be two months before the entire lake would freeze enough for Richard to drive Mark's jeep on it, but we'd have another month when it would still be navigable for a boat. I looked forward to Thanksgiving, the day he promised he'd leave Mark's boat at Goodhue's and hitch a ride to the island on one of their boats. He'd stay until the lake froze solid. On New Year's Day, he'd use the snowmobile to get across the lake, start staying in town again, cooking brunch at the Wolfeboro Inn.

When I came into the house, Jane was sitting at the table doing her morning Jumble and someone was in the kitchen burning toast. Dottie, I assumed. She liked her toast almost black. "Hard or easy today?" I said when Jane looked up at me.

"Hard. Not a good sign."

"You'll get it." I climbed the stairs to the hallway of bedrooms. After I checked on Thelma, I'd offer Stella a massage. Someone was in the bathroom at the other end of the hall. When I saw Thelma's door open, I assumed Dottie or Jane had unlatched it. I looked inside. The orange pumpkin costume lay on top of her dresser. Her toiletries were beside it and her towels still hung on the towel rack. She'd need them, so I picked them up, went down the hallway, and knocked on the bathroom door with its painting of a Dali-like melting toilet that Lucy had created. "Thelma," I called, loud enough for her to hear.

"It's Lucy. Thelma must be downstairs. Her door's open."

More than the cold morning invaded my bones. I rushed back to Thelma's room, dropped her things, and took the stairs two at a time.

"Have you seen Thelma?" I asked Jane, who was still puzzling out the Jumble.

"Her door was open when I came downstairs. I think she's in the bathroom."

"She's not." I went into the kitchen, hoping to find her instead of Dottie burning toast. Later, I'd lecture everyone about not letting Thelma in the kitchen alone. Thelma wasn't there. Only Dottie, pouring herself a cup of coffee.

"Have you seen Thelma? She's not upstairs."

"Isn't her room locked?"

"Something's wrong. We need to find her." Fear penetrated further into my bones.

"Search the house. I'll look outside." I pushed open the

door and called. "Thelma. Thelma." Only a mourning dove answered me.

I walked around the house, around the cottage, along the shoreline to the little beach where Thelma liked to swim. She was nowhere. I calmed down when I remembered how she liked the pumpkins on the dock. I left the beach and walked back to it, expecting to find her sitting among the pumpkins. As I got closer, I could see that she wasn't there. Neither were the mallards that swam around most mornings. The pumpkins had been moved to the edge of the dock, all facing the side where the water was too shallow for the boat.

Before I could walk onto the dock, I saw her. In water that was iced around her, her hair the color of the ice, her bare feet touching the sand, her back rigid beneath her white nightgown.

I dragged her out of the water, turned her over. She held her swim goggles wrapped around her dead hands.

Dottie opened the white box that held Thelma's ashes. When she filled an ice cream scoop with some, I was the only one who saw the irony. She dumped them into an urn carved out of a piece of granite from the island. The letters UNH were etched and stained blue on the irregular surface. Only after Thelma's death did I learn that the piece of granite sitting on the fireplace hearth wasn't decorative. They'd had it made when they first created their island commune. Each of them would have ashes mixed into it.

Dottie put the ice cream scoop into the box and handed it to Richard, who'd brought the ashes last night. "We'll scatter some at the dock and some on the beach then bury the rest in our island graveyard."

We put on the coats and hats and gloves that we'd dropped along the dining room table, and followed Richard outside. It was a cold morning, damp in a November fog that seemed to weep over the first of these women to die. We walked to the edge of the dock, none of us looking at the spot where Thelma had walked into the water. Paper-thin ice stretched into the lake. Richard would be able to use the boat he'd rented from Goodhue's for only a few more weeks.

He opened the box. One by one, we took off a glove and dropped a handful of ashes onto the ice. The wind blew just enough to swirl the gray ashes across the icy surface. A loon swooped low as if to honor what had been Thelma, then flew away.

At the beach where Thelma loved to swim, Richard kicked through enough ice to make a hole. This time the water sucked each handful of ash under the ice. Loons screeched from the nest they'd soon abandon, migrating to the coast and water that wouldn't freeze, leaving their young to find their way to them before the lake was fully frozen.

We started along the path that led us to the grove of oaks and maples that Dottie had designated the island graveyard. The trees were barren, the leaves that had burst into the brilliant reds and oranges of fall now brown and frost-covered on the ground. Two small gravestones were set in the ground, one marking Jonathan Edwards, the other Charles Edwards. A place was reserved for another that would one day read James Edwards. Beneath Charles's name, Dorothy Beaulieu Edwards was carved, the middle name acknowledging her French Canadian ancestry. A stone cutter had come yesterday and chiseled other names into a boulder. Thelma. Barb. Lucy. Stella. Jane. No surnames, no dates, just a memorial that they had chosen instead of burials in family plots. They would die united as they had lived at the end of their lives.

Dottie opened the Bible she'd been holding and read from Genesis, "For dust you are and to dust you shall return." We each took a handful of Thelma's ashes and dropped them into the hole that Richard had dug through the half-frozen soil in front of the boulder. Dottie took the box from Richard and turned it over. The remaining ashes spilled out in a stream of dust. Each of us threw a shovel of dirt into the hole until it was covered. When the ground thawed in spring, Thelma's daughter would come to honor her. We'd plant a clump of ferns to mark the first death that came to these long-lived women.

When we finished burying Thelma's ashes, we stood in silence, shivering against the wind that had picked up. I held Richard's hand as I looked around at the women. Which of them had unlatched Thelma's door? No one had confessed. Perhaps no one remembered. I tried to convince myself that I'd latched it tight. Whether she was lucid or confused, Thelma had walked into the water alone, but

I couldn't shake the feeling that someone had made the walk possible.

Jane was at the table looking through a photograph album. When she saw me, she said, "I hate Thanksgiving."

"Why? It's my favorite holiday."

She motioned me to sit next to her. The album was open to a black-and-white photo of a middle-aged man holding a fork and a carving knife, a turkey glowing on the counter next to him. I imagined it a golden brown instead of the gray of the photograph.

"Your father?"

Jane nodded.

"He has a wonderful smile. Is this Thanksgiving?"

"Last time I saw him alive. We had our usual family dinner. My parents, my grandmother, my brother and sister, my aunt and uncle and two cousins. I can still hear my uncle teasing my grandmother that she didn't put enough nuts in the stuffing."

"You'll like Richard's stuffing. He uses plenty of walnuts." The smell of roasting turkey had filled the house and I could hear Richard in the kitchen.

"Last year we all argued about how to make the stuffing. I suppose we'll never cook a Thanksgiving dinner again. All things pass. Like my father." She ran her hand along the photo. "That was the last day I saw him. He had a heart attack that night. Now whenever I see a turkey I remember going into his study and finding him dead in the chair he liked to read in. His eyes were open and drool was still wet on the side of his chin."

She turned the page to another black-and-white photo of her family posed in front of a window that looked out on a rhododendron bush, its leaves curled up in the cold. "My dad took this picture before we sat down to dinner. I remember how cold it was. The next day it snowed. Our minister walked to the house to help us with funeral arrangements. Everyone in this photo is dead now. When you're as old as I am, you get used to the dying."

"Your son's still alive. Have you called him today?"

"Not yet." She paged through photos, of herself cheerleading at UNH, of her and the women I now knew as old, of her and the man I recognized as her husband from the wedding photo she kept on her dresser. It was the only photo she had room for and she'd set it next to a wooden urn that held his ashes.

Gradually the photos in her book turned from black-and-white to color. She stopped at a page with her husband—Steven she'd told me—and a young boy. I would have thought it was Steve Junior except that he was Black.

"I recognize your husband. Who's the little boy?"

"Our son."

I studied the photo. Jane's husband had been blond, Scandinavian like his last name, Iverson. I looked from the photo to Jane whose wrinkled skin was clearly white.

"Adopted?"

"That's what we told people. No one here knows the story. Even Steve thinks he was adopted. When he wanted to find his birth parents, I was glad that in those days adoption records were closed."

I waited while she turned a few more pages. All held photos of her and Steven and their Black child. However this child came to be, he was obviously loved. Still was, judging from the weekly phone calls he had with his mother.

She closed the photo book. "Want to hear the story?"

I did, but I didn't want to appear too eager. "Only if you want to tell it."

She held her palm against the book as if it could help her conjure memories. "We were living in The Hague. Steven was a lawyer, working at the World Court. Those were the heady early days when we thought the Court would help bring peace to the world. Steven wasn't a judge, but he knew many of their aides. One was from Ethiopia. He was a single man, lonely away from home the same way I was."

She opened the book again to a page that showed her and Steven at some kind of beach party. She pointed to a tall Black man facing the ocean. "That's the day I told Steven I was pregnant. By then we knew he was infertile. I loved him. I was just lonely and Meleak brought me a couple afternoons of comfort. He returned to Ethiopia a month later. I never told him I was pregnant. Steven and I made up the story and we returned to New Hampshire after our baby was born. Steven set up his law practice and when Steve was old enough I started to teach second grade."

I noticed the "our." "No one ever found out?"

"You're the only one who knows. I guess I don't want

to die without someone hearing my secret. Steven was a wonderful husband and a wonderful father. We were a family."

She closed the book. "I'm going upstairs to call Steve. Tell him Happy Thanksgiving."

"Will he visit you soon?"

"Maybe. He hates New Hampshire. It was hard for him growing up as the only Black kid in Concord. I think that's why he never had kids. They hurt too much."

Jane left me to think about what she'd confided. Plain Jane's life had been far from plain and the post-World War II years had been far from the placid time I'd imagined. I went into the kitchen to help Richard. He was elbow deep into potato peelings. I wrapped my arms around his waist and kissed the back of his neck. If I gave birth to a child not his, would he stay with me? It was a foolish thought. The only man I ever saw these days was Richard.

Snow started to fall on Christmas Eve. Richard cut a tree from a stand of pines on the south end of the island. Dottie supplied the lights and wax hand molds of her boys that she made every year until they became teenagers. The others rescued favorite ornaments when they broke up the houses they lived in before committing to Heron Island.

I missed my parents who I talked with in the morning when they were finishing their celebration in Edinburgh. Not that we ever had traditional home Christmases. Their idea for Christmas was to take me on a trip so I wouldn't brood about being an only child. I'd toured museums in Paris, skied in Austria, snorkeled in Belize. Santa Claus found me even in Lapland where he'd left a doll and a doctor kit. We didn't see Santa or his sleigh, but I still remembered seeing the Northern Lights. Now as we hung decorations, I felt as if I were with a joyous gathering of great-grandmothers who had materialized in a place I was learning to call home.

Stella hung her ornament, a reindeer her daughter had sent some year she'd been traveling in Sweden. She found a place on a low scraggly branch and said, "I call her Cynthia. When she was little, Arty always made sure he wasn't selling Coca Cola products in some country that would have been better off importing orange juice. We'd name our ornaments and I'd remember why I stayed married."

Jane hung a UNH cheerleader she'd gotten from some long ago reunion. "I should never have introduced you to Farty Arty."

Stella flicked Jane's cheerleader so it danced on the tree. "Our marriage was okay. Not a close one, but he was a good father and he let me do what I wanted."

"Did you want to have a fling?" Jane stopped the ornament from dancing. For a moment I thought she was going to tell the others about her own affair.

"Not interested," said Stella.

Jane ran commentary for the other decorations. When Lucy hung up a crystal stocking, she said it glittered like diamonds. "Diamonds are forever, just like our marriages were." Barb hung a felt Santa Claus. Jane touched the face and said she'd spent years looking for a dark skinned Santa to make her son feel better. Her usual humor was turning to melancholy. Christmas was nostalgic. They all missed the past.

Earlier we'd rummaged through Thelma's room and found a plastic replica of The Old Man in the Mountain. Dottie hung it at the top of the tree and said, "We miss you, Thelma."

Richard and I contributed our collection of glass birds. We'd been exchanging them and planned to collect them until there were too many for a tree. When all the ornaments were hung, we made garlands of popcorn, transforming the tree we named Charlie Brown into something magical.

The ice between Heron Island and Wolfeboro was finally frozen enough for the snowmobile so for Christmas Eve we didn't have to rely on what was stored in the freezer. Richard made us a tenderloin that he roasted with brussels sprouts, potatoes, and carrots. I was glad to be done with canned vegetables, but I knew the frozen lake meant that Richard would begin staying in Wolfeboro again.

After dinner, everyone left a present under the tree for the morning. The women had drawn names before Thanksgiving and we made a special trip into Wolfeboro to buy gifts. Richard and I bought for each other. I put his package under the tree, a zippered wool sweater boxed and wrapped in paper decorated with snowflakes. It would give him an extra layer when he had to cross the lake on the snowmobile. Whatever he bought me wasn't clothing. The package was small. I never wore jewelry, but I suspected it was some kind of necklace I'd pretend to like.

When the last gift was placed, Barb handed out sheets with the words to Christmas carols. She began to sing "Deck the Halls" a capella. Her tongue was sharp, but her voice was a rich alto. The others followed along, Stella and Lucy off-key, Jane and Dottie with the cracking voices of age. Richard sang baritone over the dissonance while I mouthed the words because I couldn't carry a tune, especially when there was no music accompaniment. We went through "Hark! The Herald Angels Sing," "We Three Kings," and "Good King Wenceslas," ending with the figgy pudding of "We Wish You a Merry Christmas."

"Chef Richard," said Jane in the way she had been teasing him for the last few weeks. "What's a figgy pudding?"

"A pudding made with eggs and bread crumbs and lots of dried fruits, but oddly never figs. It used to be made with meats, but now it's more of a dessert doused in brandy. I'll be making some for the New Year's Brunch at the Wolfeboro Inn."

Dottie gave her music sheet to Barb and stepped in front of Richard and me. "You're really going back to living in Wolfeboro? Leaving this wife of yours?"

He put his arm around my waist. "Not leaving her. The arrangement worked in the fall. It will work in the winter. Even better when I can drive a car on the lake. I'll get us all supplied for spring. But first, Nataki and I have a date with a snowstorm."

We went outside to snow that was falling heavily. It

was coming down fast and straight. I bent and picked up a handful, ignoring the cold on my bare hands. The snow was powdery and in the light by Dottie's door I could see the soft shapes of the flakes. Unless more moisture came in the night, we wouldn't be making a snow Santa Claus. I imagined five ninety-year-old women lying on the ground making snow angels.

We walked to the dock. The snowmobile was on the ice, covered with a tarp. Richard took hold of my hands. He blew on them with the warmth of his breath. "It's beautiful here. I wish we owned an island where we could live without a flock of needy old women."

"You could stay."

He wrapped his arms around me. "By the end of this week, I'll be ready to burn the place down. I like us better when I don't feel them constantly watching."

"When spring comes, I'll think about telling them to find another nurse for a couple of days a week. I can't abandon them in the dead of winter."

"Promise?"

"I promise we'll have a lovely Christmas tomorrow." That was as close as I could manage.

"As long as we don't have to do more singing. Stella's voice was painful."

"It's no worse than mine."

"But you're more beautiful. Especially with snow in your hair." He let go of my hands and brushed away some flakes. "We'd better go in. Snuggle under the covers before we freeze to death."

As we moved off the dock, I looked at the snow piling up on the ice where I had found Thelma drowned. She was the first. If I left in the spring would someone else have died? They were old. Statistics told me what my heart didn't. "Race you." I ran toward the cottage and the comfort of knowing that Richard and I would have years ahead of us when this experiment in caretaking was over.

I woke with the dawn. The snow had stopped and the horizon was ribboned with shades of red. I dressed quickly and kissed Richard on the forehead. "I'm going to build a fire and give Stella a Christmas morning massage." He blinked, then turned onto his side. He'd be awake when I came back and we could shovel together.

I had to push hard to get the door open. Snow had covered our tracks from last night. Before I went outside, I found the yardstick someone had stored in the front closet. Maybe that someone was as compelled to measure the snowfall as I'd been growing up. I closed the door behind me and sunk deep into the powder. I stuck the yardstick into the snow. Nineteen inches. I felt a kind of irrational triumph. The sun made the snow glisten and the sky had turned a brilliant blue. I could hear the silence.

I left the yardstick in the undisturbed snow and enjoyed each step into the deep softness. The upstairs of the house blocked some of the snow, so the kitchen door opened easily. I took off my boots and hung my jacket on the step stool Stella used when she needed to reach something in a cabinet. There were no chairs, no table. The kitchen was for cooking, the dining room for eating. I went through the dining room into the living room where the Christmas tree stood with the gifts wrapped beneath it.

I recoiled at what I saw.

Stella lay on her side where she had landed at the base of the stairs. My nurse's instinct directed me to the body to check her pulse. My hand shook when I touched her neck. I leaned my ear to her heart, my hand to her nose. No beat, no breath. She was dead. I could see where a fragile bone in her neck was knocked out of place. I picked up a wooden Santa Claus that lay broken beside her. Had she been carrying it downstairs as a Christmas surprise? Or had someone else left it on the stairs to carry it down in the morning? It didn't matter. I ran up the stairs to wake Dottie and to call 911.

A coroner's team had come to the island on Christmas Day to pronounce Stella dead of an accidental fall that broke her neck. They loaded her onto a toboggan that they pulled behind a snowmobile to the funeral home in Wolfeboro.

A week later, Richard brought her ashes back to the island. He stood with us now as Dottie used the same ice cream scoop to drop some of Stella's ashes into the urn with Thelma's. She read from the same passage of Genesis that she'd read at the island graveyard. There'd be no scattering or burial of ashes in snow that was as deep as it had been on Christmas morning. In the spring, Stella's daughter would return from where we'd located her in Singapore. I looked at the four remaining women, Jane with her hypotension, Barb with arrhythmia, Lucy with diabetes. Despite her slight dowager's hump and her one deaf ear, only Dottie had managed to reach her nineties with no prescription drug. They were all about to turn ninety-three and I feared that we'd be adding more ashes to the urn before the snow melted and the ground thawed.

"Amen," said Dottie as she put the box of remaining ashes on the hearth next to the urn. "I shouldn't have teased her about Arty," said Jane.

Barb comforted her. "Stella didn't mind. We all called him Art the Fart. I think she found it affectionate."

"I never understood their marriage," said Lucy. "He was always talking about the places he'd been. The Great Wall of China, the Singapore Zoo, the pyramids. He should have taken Stella on those trips."

"She would have hated them," said Dottie.

I remembered my conversation with Stella about how she had insisted that she not be a burden on her daughter. "I admired her. She didn't resent that her daughter became a traveler."

"Stella didn't have a selfish bone in her body." Dottie pointed to the Christmas gifts that were still wrapped under the tree. "She'd want us to open these. She loved Christmas. That's why she was carrying the wooden Santa Claus down the stairs. It was too heavy."

Jane went over to the Christmas tree where Dottie had shoved the broken pieces of the Santa Claus into the box of kindling. "I thought it was your Santa Claus."

"It is. I left it just outside my door nowhere close to the stairs," said Dottie. "I was going to ask Richard to carry it downstairs. I don't know why Stella was so foolish to try. I always sleep on my good ear, so I didn't hear her come through my room or I would have stopped her."

Jane touched a piece of the broken Santa Claus. "Richard should take this away when he takes out the Christmas tree. I can't keep looking at it."

"I'll take it back to Wolfeboro, then you won't have to see it anywhere on the island. You should open these now so I can take out the tree." Richard picked up one of the Christmas gifts and read the tag. "To Barb from Lucy."

Barb took the package and unwrapped what was obviously a book. It was a collection of poetry by Margaret Atwood. She hugged Lucy in a warm gesture I hadn't seen her use since I'd come to the island. "*Dearly.* This is a perfect choice, late poems, many of them about late in life. She dedicated it to her partner who died of dementia. I'll think of Thelma when I read it."

We went slowly through the other packages. Yarn and a pattern for making socks for Jane from Barb. A knitted scarf for Dottie from Jane.

Richard picked up one of the last two gifts the women had chosen for each other. He handed it to Lucy. "It's from Stella."

Lucy slowly untied the ribbon to find a box of fancy toiletries. Handmade soap, bubble bath, skin cream, and an assortment of different color nail polishes."

"No hair dye?" said Barb.

Lucy glared at her. "Chestnut is better than the gray you all have."

Jane lightened their exchange. "Remember how we used to tease Lucy? She dyed her hair so many different colors we didn't know what her real color was."

"You'll never know what it was. And you'll never see it gray."

"Except at the roots," said Barb.

Lucy ignored her. She held a bar of soap to her nose. "Lavender." She kissed it and said, "Thank you, Stella."

Richard and I picked up our gifts to each other and opened them simultaneously. He put on the sweater I'd chosen for him. It fit perfectly over the thin Henley he was wearing. I opened the box that looked like it would contain jewelry, preparing myself to say I liked whatever piece he'd chosen. I was wrong. The gift was a pair of tickets to see *Hamilton* when it came to Boston in February.

"He asked me," said Dottie. "You deserve a night away. The four of us can survive. Enjoy a romantic escape."

"A day of wine and roses," said Lucy, forgetting that the movie with that title was about lovers whose romance descended into alcoholism.

Dottie picked up the last present from under the Christmas tree. "I'll give this to Stella's daughter when she comes for our service."

Lucy smelled another bar of soap. "Lemon. Do we get to know what you bought for her?"

"I'll keep it for a surprise. Take your decorations off the

tree so Richard can put it outside. The nuthatches will love the popcorn."

We took off the decorations we'd put up what seemed like months ago. Dottie took the wooden reindeer that had been Stella's contribution and put it with the gift box that had been meant for her. When the tree was bare of ornaments, Richard lifted it from its stand. I opened the door for him and watched him disappear around the side of the house. It wouldn't take long for the tree to be stripped of its popcorn. It would lie dead in a grove, recycled into the earth we stole it from.

By St. Patrick's Day, the island was mud-luscious. Richard had driven to it on a snowmobile laden with ingredients to cook us corned beef and cabbage. The ice was thin and I was relieved when he made it across. He was stranded now until Goodhue's could get Dottie's boat out of storage and deliver it to us. The ice was already melting as fast as a glacier in the Arctic.

I found a green sweater to wear with my jeans and left the cottage to see if I could help Richard. Everything was in one pot so he wouldn't need me, but I wanted to be near him. His visits had been sporadic since the Valentine's Day escape we'd taken to Boston to see *Hamilton*. He was more and more anxious to have me bequeath Heron Island to some other nurse.

I opened the door to the smell of corned beef and cabbage. Only Richard was Irish and only one quarter, but on St. Patrick's Day our whole country forgot its history of "No Irish Need Apply" and claimed a heritage. I could hear Lucy and Barb in the dining room arguing. The tension between them had been erupting more and more over the dark days of winter.

I kissed Richard, who was taking an Irish soda bread out of the oven. "How long have they been fighting?"

"Not long. I don't know how you've managed with those two all winter. All I asked them to do is set the table. Maybe you can calm them down."

"I'll settle them. They're excited. Barb wants us all to sing 'Danny Boy.'"

"'Finnegan's Wake' would be better."

I gave Richard a soft punch on the arm and went into the dining room. Lucy and Barb faced each other across the table, each in front of their color-coded placemats. Lucy at the red one looked like she was about the throw a plate while Barb at the blue one held a fork like a weapon.

"Put those things down and come into the living room. It's time for you to settle whatever's been bothering you." I sounded like a parent separating siblings who argued. The way they looked at me made me fear they were following Thelma into dementia.

They came with me into the living room and sat in the separate chairs that stood at right angles to the sofa. In Kelly green sweaters they could have been twins except that Barb's hair was gray and Lucy's only gray at the roots. Lucy's face looked like a blank canvas next to Barb's line drawing of wrinkles.

Lucy picked at the fingernails she'd painted green. "She never knew we found out."

I waited for one of them to explain. Barb spoke first. "She's talking about Thelma. That night in Grant's. It was St. Patrick's Day and it was Howard who hit Ryan."

"Ryan was the policeman," said Lucy. "The one I was dating."

"Only behind my back. I was dating him first." Barb spoke to me more than to Lucy.

"Is that what's been bothering you two? A long ago rivalry over some man neither of you married."

Barb said, "I couldn't marry him" at the same time that Lucy said, "He was Catholic."

"You married other men. You had families. You had good lives." I knew that they both had children and grandchildren and great-grandchildren. I'd met some of them when they visited before we got iced in. Barb and Lucy had chosen to live on Heron Island. They weren't neglected old women.

"I don't know why you can't let it go." Lucy played with one of her diamond rings.

"You're the one who can't let it go."

"Is that what you've been thinking?"

"What else would I think?" said Barb. "Ever since we moved here, you've been staying away from me unless the others are with us. Sometimes I think you were having an affair with my husband, too."

Lucy stopped playing with her ring. "Don't be ridiculous. I didn't find him attractive."

"Did you sleep with Ryan? Is that why he dropped me? Went with someone who'd have sex?"

Lucy got out of her chair and stood over the urn as if she were about to have a conversation with Thelma and Stella. She turned around to speak. "You know we were all virgins when we married. Except Dottie and that priest of hers. It's not like today. So no, Barb, I never slept with Ryan. It's not about him. It's about that day we graduated."

"What happened then? All I remember about graduation is that it poured and our caps and gowns smelled like mildew."

"It was afterwards. We were in Alpha Xi."

Barb explained to me. "Alpha Xi Delta. The sorority where we all met and became friends." She waited a moment then said, "I remember. That was the day you passed out. Why would that make you angry with me?"

Lucy returned to her chair. She clasped her hands together and closed her eyes for a moment. When she opened them, she said, "I've never told anyone this. I had one of those near-death visions. Just like the ones you read about. There was a tunnel and a bright light and a figure at the end of the tunnel telling me it wasn't my time."

"That was a good thing," said Barb. "You didn't die and you found out you have diabetes."

"Diabetes isn't good. The figure was. It was Ryan. But you weren't good. When I woke up, you were standing over me. I still remember your smile. Like you hoped I was dead. Then you could have Ryan."

This time it was Barb who got out of her chair. She

reached down and pulled Lucy to her. "I didn't want you dead. What you saw wasn't a smile. I was terrified."

"I wasn't terrified. I'm not afraid of dying. That light still comforts me."

I took hold of their hands and we formed a circle. "You've been friends forever. Remember that. It's more than most people get."

"At our age." Barb turned away from us, trying to hide the tear that had found its way from beneath her glasses into the tunnel of her deepest wrinkle.

After too much salty corned beef, too much green beer, and too many off-tune Irish songs, I'd fallen asleep in the comfort of Richard's arms. I woke while it was still dark, got up to use the bathroom, then went into the kitchen for a glass of water. Through the window above the sink, I could see a sky bright with a full moon and a gazillion stars. The silhouettes of pine trees watched over this section of the island.

I glanced at my cell phone that was charging on the counter. 5:17. Later than I thought. The sky would start to lighten in another hour. If I went back to bed, I'd toss around worrying about how long Richard and I could last with our arrangement. I'd grown to love these women, but I needed a social life beyond an elderly commune on an isolated island.

I went back into the bedroom where Richard lay dead to the world. Instead of crawling next to him, I opened the closet and took out my socks and sneakers and jacket. No one would care if I wore my pajamas to watch the sun rise from Dottie's porch.

The path to the house was lighted by the moon, empty of the snow I'd trudged through that horrible Christmas night. When I entered the kitchen, I saw the bottle of orange juice Lucy was supposed to take to her room in case her blood sugar plummeted in the night. Richard had replenished her supply of ten-ounce bottles. She took one out of the refrigerator every night and returned it, unopened, most mornings. Only a couple of times had she needed some. But she and Barb had celebrated the end of the tension between them by drinking too much beer. I was sure I'd reminded Lucy not to forget her juice. She'd be fine, I told myself, and put it into the refrigerator. When she woke, I'd give her my lecture about alcohol and blood sugar.

I went onto the porch and sat waiting for the first sounds of the morning birds and the first threads of sunrise. Richard found me just as the dome of sun appeared over the lake. He handed me a mug of coffee. "You couldn't sleep. Anything wrong?"

"I drank too much. And I'm brooding."

"About what?"

"Us. Them. You're right. I need more than an isolated life on an island caring for four old women."

The high screech of a loon sounded from the edge of the island. "They're back," said Richard. "A signal. It's time for us to leave the island."

"We signed a contract. Besides, they need us and I like them.

"You do more house cleaning than nursing."

He was right. Since Thelma and Stella died, I'd begun to help by vacuuming and dusting and cleaning the bathrooms. At least they still did their own laundry. "I've been thinking of a plan," I said.

"And it is?" said Richard.

The sun was fully risen and the songbirds were in full chorus as if they were approving of the plan I described. "I'll ask Dottie to hire a nurse for two days a week. On the other days, I'll stay on the island and you can come to do whatever Dottie asks for. We can stay in Mark and Meredith's house until they come for the summer. We'll figure something out after that."

"There's something I haven't told you."

"It's bad." I was afraid that he was going to tell me he'd found a job in Boston.

"Not at all. Your plan can work. The Wolfeboro Inn is giving me more hours as soon as the summer season starts. I've been negotiating a room as part of my salary."

"I love you," I said as I took hold of his hand. "I'll ask Dottie today." We sat quietly until I heard the first sound of someone rummaging in the kitchen.

"I'm going inside to check on everyone, then I'll get dressed. After the Mindful Movement session, we can both talk to Dottie."

I found Dottie and Jane in the kitchen. I opened the cabinet where I kept medicines and gave Jane her ludrocortisone.

She swallowed it with coffee. "You know I can remember these pills myself."

"But you never remember to take a pill with water." I filled a glass for her and one that I'd carry upstairs for Barb along with her morning pill. I found Lucy's insulin and her monitor.

As I started for the stairs, Dottie said, "Barb's in the bathroom. Lucy's door is still closed. They both drank too much yesterday."

"So did I. What's it mean that I can't keep up with you ladies?"

"We love you anyway," Jane called after me.

Barb was just coming out of the bathroom, a blue towel wrapped around her. She held an arm out to me. "Chicken skin, we call it. I wish I had a face with as few wrinkles as Lucy's. Thank you for yesterday. I had no idea why I've been bothering her so much."

I gave Barb her pill and the glass of water. "I'll check on Lucy. She forgot her orange juice last night."

"No she didn't. I watched her take it out of the refrigerator." She closed the door to her bedroom as if she was afraid I'd see more of her wrinkled body.

I knocked on Lucy's door. No answer so I knocked again. Still no answer so I opened it.

Lucy was on her stomach, her arm stretched out of her red comforter toward the nightstand where she should have found her orange juice. I rushed to the bed and felt for a pulse the way I'd felt for Stella's. There was none. I wanted to lie beside her and cry, but my nursing instinct took over. I found her cell phone and dialed 911 for the third time since we'd settled on the island in July.

After a month living with only three other women, on Easter I felt like I was in a crowd. Richard was planting ferns in front of what I'd begun to call the burial boulder. Three deaths. An unlatched door, a fall, a missing bottle of orange juice. I planted my uneasiness with the fern I was putting over Thelma's ashes.

Stella's and Lucy's families had arrived for the burial. Lucy's two children with their spouses, five grandchildren with more spouses, and their children who were old enough to give Lucy great-grandchildren all scooped ashes into the hole in front of her name. If they resented that Lucy had chosen to spend her last days on Heron Island, they didn't say. I'd told them about Lucy's near-death experience, embellishing it not with an unfulfilled romance but with an assurance that she hadn't been afraid to die. Ever since I found her dead, I'd wondered who beckoned her into the white light.

Dottie handed the gift she'd bought at Christmas to Stella's daughter. Cynthia carefully unwrapped it. She handed the box to her husband and held up the heavy glass heron meant for her mother. She dropped it into the hole on top of Stella's ashes and said, "This is for Heron Island and your friendships." She moved back to her husband and let Richard place the last fern in the ground. Three ferns that would spread over three women and mark the vitality of their lives.

Dottie spoke the words from Genesis, then opened her Bible to another verse. "These are words Jesus spoke about raising Lazarus from the dead. 'I am the resurrection and the life; whoever believes in me, even if he dies, will live.' Thelma, Stella, and Lucy won't rise physically, but it's Easter. We should all believe in resurrection."

No one argued. I knew only that these women would live in my memory until I died.

We walked silently back to the house and the Easter brunch Richard was preparing. As we passed the little beach where Thelma loved to swim, a heron swooped down and stood on the shore, scattering the ducks that had claimed the spot as their favorite. I stopped with Richard to watch it until it dipped its head in the water. "You need to talk with Dottie about an extra nurse before these women become real patients, not just lonely old women wanting a companion." He sounded wistful as the heron rose with a fish in its mouth then silently took flight toward its rookery.

"We used to call it Easter Monday." Dottie poured herself coffee and picked up a plate with ham and a colored Easter egg left over from yesterday's brunch. She handed me a plate. "Have some. After all, it's your husband who made it."

I accepted quickly. This was my chance to talk with her about a second nurse. "Thanks. I'll eat with you before I take medicine to Barb and Jane."

"Guess I'm the only hardy one left. Like those peas we'll plant this afternoon."

We carried our plates into the dining room. "Why Easter Monday?" I said as I cut into a piece of ham.

"Charles taught me the phrase. When he was at Boston College, they always had a long holiday, Thursday through Monday. They didn't want students having to drive back to campus on Easter Sunday."

"When I was in nursing school, we didn't have any kind of Easter holiday." Part of me wished for a simpler society where families could gather and pretend that all Americans believed in the resurrection of Christ. I studied her pale face and realized that I hadn't seen any brown or black skin since I'd come to Heron Island. Richard was right. We needed time away. "Speaking of long weekends," I said.

"You want time off." She began to peel her hardboiled egg. The white flesh had streaks of red from the dye we used to color it. "I hear you and Richard talking. You can't leave us."

"I don't want to. We just want two days in a row so we can have more time together. You don't really even need a nurse."

"We need company. None of us ever lived alone. That's why we came here. Live together, die together."

Her comment chilled me. If I left, would they all follow Thelma and drown in Lake Winnipesaukee? "There are still three of you. I'm betting you'll all reach a hundred."

"Not likely. It's okay. We've made arrangements."

I slowly peeled my egg as if I were peeling away whatever concealed some secret Dottie was hiding. "Do I get to hear the arrangements?"

"You should know them. After Thelma died, the rest of us talked. We'll stay here until there's only one of us left. We want to keep you here. It helps with the loneliness."

I pictured myself nursing two more women to their deaths. Their loneliness would become mine. "What then?"

"Unless I'm completely decrepit, I'll go to Sugar Hill. Nice assisted living. That's the real last exit, not Heron Island." She assumed she would outlive Barb and Jane.

"What if you're not the last one left?"

"Then someone else will go to Sugar Hill. James will come back. He's going to open a retreat center on Heron Island. Already planning it as if he's planning for us to die soon. I won't mind it. I'll get to see him. And you'll get to leave. But not yet. We need you."

Again she assumed she'd be the last to die. "No one's dying yet," I said.

"We're making it worth your while. Whatever's left of the money the others have been pooling to maintain this arrangement will be yours. James won't need it. He'll get my money and the Catholic church will support his retreat center."

She was making me feel trapped. "We don't expect money and I really need to have time off. You can reduce my salary."

"It's not about money. You're the one who keeps us from being lonely. Not that husband of yours, but he does his job."

"You all kept your marriages together for more years than I've been alive. I want mine to last that long."

"Find us someone and I'll see." She picked up her coffee cup and drank. "Coffee's stronger than tea. I'll be the last one standing."

As April moved softly into May, the lettuce and spinach and peas sprouted. On Mother's Day while Richard worked at the Wolfeboro Inn, we added everything except sensitive tomatoes and basil. I handed a packet of bean seeds to Dottie, cucumber to Jane, and summer squash to Barb. We wore the hats we'd worn when we were on the *Mount Washington* what seemed like years ago. I was comfortable in an old pair of jeans and the others wore long dresses and worn-out sneakers. They looked like sharecropper women.

I turned over the cultivator hoe. "Never leave tines pointing up. That's how Richard got his scar."

"If we fell on it, a scar wouldn't make us look sexy," said Jane.

"You did get a handsome one," said Barb as she pushed a squash seed into the ground.

Only Dottie hadn't warmed to Richard.

I opened the package of pumpkin seeds. I wanted to still be on Heron Island when the pumpkins grew large enough for jack-o'-lanterns.

Jane finished with the squash seeds first. She struggled to stand up.

"Wait. I'll help you." I pushed the last pumpkin seed into the earth I'd mounded for it.

When I got Jane onto her feet, she leaned against me. "Just a head rush. I must be getting old." She laughed as she managed to straighten herself.

Barb reached an arm to me, so I helped her up, too. "Must be catching. I'm a bit dizzy myself. I'm ready for a nice cup of tea."

Dottie stood up without my help. "Tea's for old ladies like you two. I'll make coffee for Nataki and me." She brushed off the front of her dress. "We've earned some of those cookies Richard brought from the Wolfeboro Inn."

Jane wiped her hands on her dress and laughed at the streaks she made. "Dress is as old as me. I like all those bread and pastries Richard brings from the Inn."

"Don't forget that honey sample he brought yesterday. He said it was the only one from Turkey. It's good. I can use some in my tea right now." Barb's voice was shaky and she seemed a little wobbly as she began walking toward the house. It was time to take all these women to see Doctor Savage.

Only Dottie was in the kitchen when I came into the house the morning after our planting. I could smell her coffee brewing and her toast burning. "Any signs of life upstairs?" I asked.

The toast popped, the only noise in the quiet house. As Dottie started to spread peanut butter on it, she said," You know I sleep on my good ear. Far as I know, we're all still alive."

I found the pill boxes. Monday. One pill for Barb from the blue box and one for Jane from the green. Jane usually greeted me with some kind of gallows humor about swallowing a lifeline with water or about a pill leading her to tea and toast and toning. She still cracked jokes and still went through Mindful Movement exercises, but the loss of their friends had sucked out some of the joy of living on Heron Island.

I put the pills and glasses of water on a tray. "Richard's coming this morning. How about we all go into Wolfeboro for lunch. My post-Mother's Day treat."

"Ask Jane and Barb. We could use a change." Dottie picked up her breakfast and carried it to the dining room.

When I reached the top of the stairs, I saw that neither Jane nor Barb had opened her door. I smiled at the caricature that hung on Barb's door. Lucy had drawn her with lines of a poem streaming out of her mouth. The drawing made me miss Heron Island's artist.

Barb's "come in" didn't sound poetic. Her voice was weaker than her usual alto. When I opened the door, I saw why. She was pale and soaked in sweat. She tried to sit up to face me. "I'm sick. Barely made it to the bathroom."

"Diarrhea? Vomiting?"

"Both. I hope I didn't leave a mess."

"Dottie's up and didn't say anything so it should be

fine. Lie back down." I set the tray on her dressing table and went to the bed to feel her forehead. "You don't seem feverish. When did this start?"

"I don't know. It was dark."

"You should have called me."

She lay back down and pulled the covers over her. "I'll be okay. Just need to sleep."

I unfolded the afghan Jane had knitted for her in the blue of Barb's color code and spread it over the comforter. "I'll see to Jane then get you some tea. It will settle your stomach."

"Thanks. You're good to us."

I picked up the tray with Jane's water and pill and carried it to the bathroom to check if there was a mess. It looked clean enough. Someone had opened the window so whatever smell there might have been was gone.

Jane didn't answer when I knocked below the caricature of her. Lucy had drawn Jane in profile and transformed her glasses to a monocle studying the letters of a Jumble that would unscramble from ENJA to JANE. I opened the door and saw that she was asleep. I set down the tray and went closer to the bed. She looked like Barb. Pale and sweaty. I could see a faint line of vomit on her pillow. She heard me and opened her eyes. "I think I'm sick."

"Barb is, too. Springtime bug probably." I'd been sick in the mornings for the last week, but I knew it wasn't a bug. I needed to find a time to tell Richard what I'd suspected since I skipped my period in April.

I touched her face. "You don't seem feverish. Go back to sleep and I'll bring you both tea in an hour. You need to stay hydrated." She could have been Barb's twin encased in green instead of blue. She turned on her side and pulled the covers over her head.

Downstairs I found Dottie still sitting at the dining room table. "Do you feel okay?" I reached my hand out to check her forehead. "Barb and Jane are both sick."

She pushed my hand away. "I'm fine. Can just you and I go to that lunch? These spring bugs last only a day. We all caught one last year. Didn't even need a nurse."

"I'll check on them in a little while. Bring them some tea. Let's wait until tomorrow for lunch. It will be more fun with all of us. Besides, Richard has the boat in Wolfeboro. I'll need to arrange with him." I went back to the cottage to fix my own breakfast. Toast, eggs scrambled with cheese, coffee. A little hardier than what ninety-year-olds ate. I had a feeling it would be a long day.

After I tidied up the cottage and myself, I picked up my medical kit and went back to the house. I wanted Barb and Jane to sleep longer, so I watched Dottie go through Mindful Movement by herself. "It's lonely," she said when she finished. "Usually the mornings go fast. It's only the late afternoons that drag. Barb writes poetry, all about growing old. Jane knits and does those Jumbles. You're the only one who'll play some game with me."

More and more she was stopping at the cottage to ask me to come to the house and play Scrabble. She took forever to make a word and the afternoon would drag on the way I saw my life dragging into a loneliness as deep as hers. Until now. I stroked my stomach and smiled.

"Without you, I'd just take naps. The last refuge of the aged." She pronounced "aged" with two syllables.

"Speaking of naps, I'm going to fix tea for Jane and Barb. See if I can get them out of bed. They'll feel better if they wash up."

In the kitchen, I found the butterfly cup Jane preferred and the one from the National Poetry Foundation that Barb liked. The mugs were stained from years of use. I fixed breakfast tea for both of them, adding two teaspoons of honey into each cup. I'd been trying all year to get them to switch to herbal tea, but they insisted on drinking black tea with honey.

I put the mugs and two tin bowls on a tray. They wouldn't have to run to the bathroom if they vomited the tea. I stopped first at Barb's room. She was sitting up staring out the window that overlooked the lake. I checked her temperature and her blood pressure and listened to her heart. Her heartbeat was irregular but no more than usual. I handed her the mug and put the bowl on the bed next to her. "Just in case. Are you feeling better?"

She inhaled the steam coming from the tea. "A little. This will help." She took a first sip.

"Jane doesn't feel well either. I'd guess food poisoning, but Dottie and I ate the same things you ate. Probably a bug like the one Dottie said you had a year ago. Drink the tea, sleep some more, and I'll come check on you at lunchtime, see if you're ready to eat something."

"You're good to us. I'm writing a poem for you. Something to leave you when I die."

"No one's dying yet. Shall I leave your door open?"

"Please."

I watched her take another sip as I crossed the hall into Jane's room. Jane was still lying down, but when she heard me, she pushed herself up and leaned against the headboard. Her blood pressure was too low. She needed to take her medicine, but she brushed away the pill I tried to give her. "Later. I'll just throw it up."

I handed her the mug of tea. After one sip, she gave it back to me. "Will you help me to the bathroom?"

"Still nauseous?" I set the tea on her nightstand.

"Just dizzy. I want to brush my teeth. My mouth tastes like a garbage can."

I took her toiletry bag from the dresser and helped her out of bed and into the bathroom. Lucy's painting of the Dali-like toilet seemed more sinister than funny. It took a long time before the toilet flushed and another long time before the water in the sink stopped running. When Jane opened the door, she was smiling. "I feel much better," she said as she handed me her bag.

I let her walk on her own to her room. She got to her bed and collapsed on it. "I'm not quite ready to get up."

"That's okay." I set down her bag, put the bowl next to her, and handed her a glass of water and her fludrocortisone. She managed to swallow the pill and accepted the mug of tea. "This will settle your stomach. I'll come back at lunchtime."

I left her door open like Barb's. As I descended the stairs, I scanned my own body. No headache, no dizziness, no feeling of unexplained nausea rising. If Barb and Jane had some kind of flu, Dottie and I would be next. I was the pregnant nurse. I couldn't catch the flu.

I spent the morning walking in circles around the island, trying to occupy myself by identifying the wildflowers that were blooming. I recognized the purple violets, the pink pouches of lady's slippers, the translucent Indian pipes. Jane was the one who knew botany. If she felt better after lunch, I'd take her for a walk. The fresh air would do her good.

I stopped in front of the granite rock that marked the names of the women of Heron Island. The ferns that had been just uncurling when we planted them were full and deeply green. I touched the women's names and imagined their lives. Thelma with her thick hair and thick body had once been young, had eaten pistachio ice cream on St. Patrick's Day and danced to music on a jukebox with the man she married. Skinny Stella had a spine strong enough to ignore that her husband had affairs and to find fulfillment in teaching and raising a daughter largely on her own. I imagined Lucy in the sky with diamonds after she accepted the hand of a figure bathed in white light at the end of a tunnel. Three women who made my life fuller for having known them. I swallowed my sadness and turned back to the house where three more women needed me.

I met Dottie on my way. She was standing at the beach,

watching a sailboat navigate through a wind that was rolling in. By evening, the lake would be choppy and rain would chase the boats into their ports. "This is a scene Lucy would like to paint," I said as I approached her.

"What made you think of her?"

"I was at the graves. I miss them."

"When you're as old as I am, you'll get used to the missing."

I put my hand around her waist. "What are you thinking about, standing here by yourself?"

"The past. Charles. Jonathan. I want to still be here when James comes back from that jungle of his."

"Maybe you can get him to come back now. At least for a visit."

"Maybe." She moved away from me. "I'm going to visit the graveyard. Are the ferns alive?"

"They're flush with life."

"Fertilized by ashes. There'll be more to come. Go check on Barb and Jane." She left me before I could ask if she'd seen them.

I hurried to the house. It was quiet inside. I climbed the stairs to ask if they felt ready to eat something. Maybe just toast with a little of the honey Richard had brought to spread on it. And water. They'd had enough black tea.

Jane was standing at her window. She turned and looked at me as if I were a stranger. "Did you take Stevie? You're not Black. Why do you want my Black child?"

"It's me, Jane. I'm Nataki. Your nurse."

She swatted at her hair. "What's a bird doing in here?"

She was hallucinating.

"Let's get you back to bed." I caught her before she fell. "Lie down now. Close your eyes. I'll come back after I check on Barb."

She rubbed her cheek. "I have a friend named Barb. Do I have wrinkles?"

"You're beautiful." I put her hands under the covers. She was as confused as if she had a high fever but her forehead was cool.

I hurried across the hall. Barb was sitting up in bed brushing something off the spread. "Fish. They're all over my bed." Her brushing got more frantic.

"You're dreaming. There are no fish. Lie down."

"Who are you?"

"Nataki. You know me." I pulled her away from the headboard and under the covers. "Go back to sleep now. You'll feel better after you rest."

I left the two women in their beds and ran to the cottage for my phone. I'd seen too many people die of Covid to wait longer for them to improve. I started to call Richard then pressed 911 instead. They'd send an emergency boat to get Jane and Barb to a hospital. Whatever they had, it wasn't a simple summer flu.

Richard, Dottie, and I sat outside the Intensive Care unit in Huggins Hospital. The furniture was institutional generic. A couple of chairs and a loveseat upholstered in muted tans. The walls were the kind of soft blue that was supposed to be calming and the few photographic prints were of scenes from the lake. Only one print, that of The Old Man in the Mountain stood out, a reminder that even this granite formation had fallen to its death.

Dottie sat on the chair opposite Richard and me on the loveseat. Her head rested on her chest, accenting her dowager's hump. She looked like some kind of sleeping reptile. I huddled close to Richard. Did Barb and Jane have something that would spread to us the way Covid had spread to so many I nursed in Boston? Were they Patients Zero in some new pandemic?

A doctor came into the waiting room and introduced herself as Doctor Hughes. Richard and I stood. Dottie jerked her head up so fast I feared she wrenched her neck. She shook herself awake and stood next to us.

Doctor Hughes spoke first. "We're assuming some kind of food poisoning. We've given them both atropine. It will help raise Jane's blood pressure and it should stabilize Barbara's heart rate. I'd say botulism but they don't have the weakness in their facial muscles that I'd expect with that. Whatever it is, we need to know, so I've ordered blood and urine samples for testing."

"Could it be a new kind of virus?"

"Not likely or you'd be showing symptoms."

Dottie's voice cracked when she said, "I'm perfectly fine. Can we see them?"

"They're both asleep. You'll be the most help if you go home. Check your refrigerator. If they have food poisoning, we need to know what it's from. Don't eat anything that doesn't come from a box or a can. Someone will call when they wake up."

"They'll be okay." Dottie's words were a statement more than a question.

"We'll call. Do you need a ride home?" Doctor Hughes looked at Richard, assuming he was in charge.

"A ride? We live on an island. All of us." Dottie's tone was hostile, as if the doctor should know about their lives. Richard calmed her. "I have your boat at Mark and Meredith's. I have their car. Come with me and we'll get the boat. Nataki will leave phone numbers for the doctor."

I could read Richard the way I was reading Dottie. She was afraid. He was leaving me to hear any bad news the doctor had been holding back.

As soon as they were out of earshot, Doctor Hughes said, "Trace yesterday for me. When did they first show symptoms?"

"It was Mother's Day and my husband was at the Wolfeboro Inn. He's a chef and was there for the brunch. He left a frittata for me to warm, so we all ate together."

"You ate the same things?"

I visualized us at the table. "Yes. The frittata had spinach and bacon in it. We all ate that and fruit salad and toast."

"Drinks?"

"Barb and Jane always drink tea. Dottie and I had coffee."

"Juice?"

"No. I was going to make mimosas but I needed to pass." She scanned my body. "Needed to?"

"I haven't told anyone yet. My morning sickness isn't from food poisoning."

"Congratulations. The nausea will pass in a few weeks."

"I know. I'm a nurse."

A middle-aged couple came in. The woman was crying and her husband was holding her up. A nurse let them into Intensive Care. I heard her say, "We've stabilized him. He's lucky that fall didn't kill him."

Doctor Hughes shook her head. "Kid came in while I was in the ED. Sometimes I wonder how patients like yours made it to ninety."

"They're my friends, not just my patients."

"Anything else you can tell me? What did you do after brunch?"

"We planted the garden. These women might be old, but they're strong."

"I hope so. Whatever they have is complicated by Jane's hypotension and Barbara's arrhythmia. Did they take their usual medicine yesterday?"

"They did."

"When you finished gardening they were okay?"

"Jane and Barb were both a little dizzy. We went back to house and had cookies that Richard brought from the Inn."

"Drinks?"

"Tea and coffee."

"What about dinner?"

"We ate leftovers. It couldn't be food poisoning or Dottie and I would be sick."

"Did they snack on something later?"

"They usually don't. When I peeked in to say goodnight and give out pills, they were watching television."

"Amiodarone for Barb and fludrocortisone for Jane?"

"Morning and night. If I don't watch them, they don't drink enough water. Only Jane took hers this morning. Are they going to be okay?"

She studied me as if she thought I'd been acting out Arsenic and Old Ladies. "I don't know. It's an interesting case. If no one calls you, call Intensive Care. I'll tell them you're the contact. You were right to bring them in. If they have family, you should call them." She left me to worry. It was never good to be an interesting case.

Waves rocked the boat and my stomach on the way back to the island. We made it before the first bolt of lightning. Richard and I secured the tarp over the boat while Dottie went into the house to call Jane's son and Barb's family.

"They should have come for Mother's Day," said Richard as he tied down the last rope.

"Jane's son avoids New Hampshire. Barb's family all had excuses. Dance recitals, school plays, baseball games. They're coming on Memorial Day."

"There might be two more women to memorialize by then."

"Don't think that way."

Another bolt of lightning struck the water. The thunder that followed brought with it the first rain. We ran to the house just in time to avoid getting drenched.

Richard opened the refrigerator. "I'll fix us some dinner."

"From a box or a can, the doctor said."

"If Barb and Jane have food poisoning, it wasn't from anything you all ate yesterday."

"Make it something bland." My stomach was rebelling after the choppy boat ride. "I'll see if Dottie wants something."

"She's probably dead to the world."

"Bad expression," I said as I left him in the kitchen hunting for something to cook and I went upstairs to check on Dottie.

He was right. She was lying on her side, her good ear settled into her pillow. Sleep was a gift. I'd check on her before Richard and I went to the cottage and collapsed into our own bed.

I went downstairs and onto the porch to wait for whatever dinner he'd made. The sky had darkened with the night as well as with the storm. I sat in the dark listening to the rain. It pounded on the roof and gushed from the storm drains. Thunder sounded in three-second intervals after each flash of lightning struck the water.

Richard came onto the porch. He set a tray on the table I'd moved between two chairs. "I'll turn on a light."

"Don't. There's enough light from the living room. The dark is nice."

"Not enough light to see what I made."

"Doesn't matter. I can taste." I found a plate on the tray.

Richard took the other plate and handed me a fork. "I expect a clear description of what you're eating."

I couldn't see it, but I could smell it. I managed to get something on my fork and into my mouth. Rotini tossed with pesto that he must have taken out of the freezer from the supply we made last summer. He'd added artichoke hearts that he found in an unopened can. Nothing that said food poisoning.

"Pasta, pesto, artichokes. You're magic."

"Not a lot to choose from."

We ate in silence, concentrating on getting the food to our mouths in the dark. I jumped every time it thundered even though I expected the noise.

Richard set down his plate and said what I'd been thinking. "This might mean that Dottie's right. She'll be the last one alive. She'll go to Sugar Hill. We'll have money and our freedom."

"Don't be mercenary. I don't want Jane and Barb to die."

"You're right. I shouldn't wish death even on ninety-year-olds. As soon as this is over, we'll find another nurse to help you. We need a couple of days a week for freedom."

I seized the opening. "There's something else that will tie us down."

"Don't tell me that Dottie's inviting in another old lady."

"Not an old one. Maybe not even a lady. I'm—"

Richard jumped out of his chair, took my tray away, and pulled me off my chair and into his lap. "You're pregnant."

"I am."

He nuzzled his face onto my neck and stroked my

stomach. "I love you," he said, then added, "I love you both."

The call had come just as the sun was rising. If we wanted to see Jane alive, we needed to get to the hospital. Richard, Dottie, and I stood now in the waiting room outside Intensive Care. A nurse came in. I could tell from her expression that we were too late. "I'm sorry," she said. "Jane didn't make it."

Dottie began to sob quietly. This was the first time she hadn't held herself together when one of her friends died.

"We have her in one of the patient rooms. You can see her before we—" She stopped. I knew what she meant. She'd call for the body to be picked up by whatever funeral parlor Dottie named.

"What about Barb?" I asked.

The nurse mouthed at me, "Not good."

Through her sobs, Dottie said, "Go see Barb. I'll meet you there."

Richard started to follow me into Intensive Care. "Just their caregiver," said the nurse. She opened the door to the unit and another nurse let me inside. I passed the young man who'd been brought in yesterday. He was immobilized on a bed.

Barb was lying behind a curtain that isolated her. She opened her eyes. Without her glasses, she looked like whatever ghostly figure had beckoned her through the tunnel. She grabbed for my hand. "Find the poem. It's for you." It was all the breath she had.

She closed her eyes. Drool appeared on the side of her mouth. I found a tissue on the stand beside her bed and wiped her mouth. The drool kept coming and her breathing became more labored. Dottie came into the room and took my place holding Barb's hand. I grabbed more tissues and went to the other side of the bed.

Dottie leaned over and put her head on Barb's chest. "Jane's dead. You can't die."

Barb opened her eyes. She managed to say, "I want to die." She closed her eyes again. The death rattle rose in her throat. Then calm. The letting go.

Dottie looked at me from across the bed. "It's over," I said.

Dottie bent and kissed Barb's wrinkled face. "We had fun, didn't we. All those years. Heron Island was a good last plan." Her voice broke and she began to sob again. This time her sobs were full and loud. Another nurse had rushed to the bedside. She'd watched as Barb took her last breath. There was nothing she could have done. She pulled Dottie gently away and said to me, "Take her home now. Someone will contact you later."

The call came in the early afternoon. Doctor Hughes wanted to meet with me. I made sure that Dottie would be okay for a couple of hours and asked Richard to come with me. I was nervous about what I'd learn. Had I missed something?

The fifteen-minute boat trip felt like half an hour.

Richard docked at the marina and we walked the two miles to Huggins Hospital. He stayed in the waiting area outside Doctor Hughes's office.

The office was the kind I'd seen all over the hospital in Boston, shared with other doctors who hung their medical diplomas on the wall.

She motioned me to sit, looked at her computer screen, then at me. "Your friends' symptoms were so strange I called the regional poison control center. I sent their ideas along with specimens to a reference lab. The tox results are more than strange. Are there azaleas or rhododendron on the island?"

"A few planted around the house. Why?" I said, anxious to hear the results.

"They had a grayanotoxin in their system. It wouldn't have been enough to kill them if both hadn't had underlying conditions."

"I'm sorry. I never heard of a grayanotoxin."

"It's a toxin in azaleas and rhododendron. Their symptoms fit, but I wouldn't have diagnosed it without a tox screen. Would they have tried to make something like an azalea tea? They could have been drinking it in small doses before the toxin overloaded their systems."

"I don't understand. They drank black tea, too much of it."

"Do you keep honey bees on the island?"

"Barb and Jane were over ninety. They didn't take up beekeeping. How would that matter?"

"If bees feed off azaleas and rhododendron, they can

produce something called Mad Honey. I had to look it up. There's none produced in the United States, but some bee keepers in Turkey market it."

"They market a poison?"

"In small amounts it won't kill anyone. They market it as an hallucinogen and an aphrodisiac."

It clicked at the same time that a Code Blue sounded over the loudspeaker. Doctor Hughes pushed back her chair. "We're checking all the stores around here that sell herbal remedies. They should be outlawed. If you have any honey, throw it out." She rushed to answer the Code Blue.

I stood for a moment before I joined Richard. He'd brought honey. The only jar from Turkey. He couldn't have known it was toxic. I brought Jane and Barb tea to settle their stomachs even after they showed symptoms.

Richard came through the open door into the office. "Well?" he said.

I looked in his eyes. He wasn't guilty. I was.

"It was food poisoning." I couldn't say anything else. Not yet.

We walked the two miles back to the marina and took the boat to the island. When he eased the boat to the dock, he didn't turn the motor off. "I need to go back to the Inn. Finish the arrangements I'm making for our future."

I watched him move the boat into the deep water of Winnipesaukee. When it was out of sight, I walked slowly up the path to the house and Dottie. I could see her on the porch. Her head was bowed in sleep. I opened the door to the kitchen quietly. The honey jar was on the counter where I'd left it after I gave Barb and Jane the final dose that led to their death. I picked it up and studied the label. The front read Pure Turkish Honey, written over a photo of the Black Sea. I looked at the back of the jar. Another photo, this one of a honeycomb. Under the photo in fine print were the words "Mad Honey. Use in small doses." No explanation why.

I dumped the jar into the trash can, tied up the plastic can liner, and took the trash that didn't need to be emptied to the can outside. Mad honey would kill no one else. Jane and Barb's deaths would be listed as hypotension and arrhythmia complicated by unexplained exposure to a grayanotoxin. Any guilt I'd carry as a secret to my grave.

Instead of a family celebration, Memorial Day brought Jane's son and Barb's family to bury their ashes. Dottie read the same Bible verse about dust to dust and the families took what few mementos they wanted. Dottie had said goodbye and was resting in the living room, exhausted from yet another burial.

I stood now with Jane's son Steve on the dock. We watched Richard pull away with Barb's family, who had overloaded the boat. I felt the irony. The Black man excluded.

"Walk to the grave with me," Steve said. "It will be quieter now." He was almost seventy, a man with more of his Ethiopian father than his Anglo mother in his height and his skin color. I could see why he believed he was adopted and why it would have been hard growing up in a state where no one looked like him.

We walked along the water, then cut into the path that led us to the graveyard. He knelt in front of the freshly planted fern that marked the spot where we laid Jane's ashes. When he stood, his eyes were wet. "I needed to tell her I knew. I like to believe she heard me."

"You knew?" My tone indicated a question I didn't want to ask directly.

"I wasn't adopted. She's my mother."

Rays of sunlight angled through the trees, dappling the fern and Jane's name on the boulder. "She told me. She wanted someone to know. How did you find out?"

"DNA. I wanted to learn something about my biological parents. I assumed their ancestry included slavery."

"You never told her? Asked who your father was?"

"It didn't matter. She was my mother and my father was my father. She must have trusted you to have shared her secret."

"It made me proud to be trusted. There's not much to tell. It happened when they were in The Hague. Your dad—Steven—worked constantly and your mother was lonely. The man was Ethiopian, an aide to a representative at the World Court. They were two lonely people in a country where they were foreigners."

"I know how that feels."

"He never knew about you."

"It wouldn't matter. My dad was my dad."

"He must have been a wonderful man."

"The best. You've been a good friend to all these women."

He touched Jane's name and said, "Goodbye, Mum. I saved some of your ashes. I'll mix them with Dad's."

We walked together to meet Richard at the dock. Steve bent to hug me then stepped into the boat. When they pulled away, I went into the house to find Dottie. She was awake in the living room, sitting on the sofa in front of the fireplace hearth and staring at the urn with the blue UNH etching. It held some of everyone's ashes but her own.

I sat next to her and put my arm around her. She stiffened. "You would have left anyway."

"I won't leave until James arrives. I'll help you move and I'll visit when you're at Sugar Hill."

"You'll have other things to do. With the baby."

I hadn't told anyone except Richard that I was pregnant. Not even my parents, who would be thrilled to have a grandchild. "How do you know about that?"

"I'm not blind. Jane and Barb know as well. We're happy for you." She spoke as if they were alive.

"All the more reason for me to visit. We like Wolfeboro. It will take time, but we plan to save enough to buy a house."

"There's plenty of money left in the Heron Island kitty. It will help you."

"The money should go to the families, not us."

"No one's family needs it. Besides, we all made out wills when we moved in together. After Thelma died, we signed an agreement about what to do with our common money if any was left. If Thelma had family, they might claim that she didn't understand what she was signing. One of Lucy's grandchildren might try to fight it, but she wouldn't win and all the money would go to a lawyer."

"It's still more generous than we deserve. Where should we donate some? UNH maybe?"

"A perfect place. But keep enough for yourself. You deserve it." She implied me, not Richard. "Consider it continued payment. For all those visits to Sugar Hill."

"I'll enjoy them. If we have a girl, I want to name her Dorothy."

She choked back a sob when she said, "I have something for you." She wiggled out of my arm and picked up a piece of paper that was lying next to the urn. "This is from Barb."

I unfolded the paper. It was a poem, the handwriting wobbly but clear.

"Read it out loud," she said. "It will make me think that Barb's still here. That they're all still here."

I took several deep breaths before I could start.

> *Here where the herons live*
> *   and the loons fly low*
> *Here where the mourning dove cries*
> *   and ducks drift quietly in the glacial*
> *   lake*
> *Here where ferns uncurl their fronds*
> *   like a fetus birthing*
>
> *Here six old women remember days*
> *   before hairless skin,*
> *and flabby arms, and*
> *   wrinkles on cadaverous faces*

*Here Nataki comes with her
      taut body, her smooth skin,
curious about loons and ferns
      and the lives of old people*

*May she remember the names carved
      on the granite boulder
May she blossom here, white and green and full
      as the mountain laurel in spring*

I hugged Dottie, who was still standing. When I released her, she wiped the tear from my cheek.

James arrived on July 1st, the anniversary of the year I'd learned to think of the island as Heron Haven. He was a kind man, almost elderly in his demeanor. I suspected that he became a missionary instead of a priest to avoid the church's celibacy rules and that he had escaped marriage because he preferred men to women. If Dottie knew, she'd kept it a secret.

I sat on the dock dangling my feet in the water while I waited for James and Richard to return from Wolfeboro where they'd brought the few things we owned to our temporary housing at the Wolfeboro Inn. Next to me, a canvas bag held a memento from each of the women I'd come to care about.

I took out Thelma's wedding ring and slipped it onto my finger. She was the first to die, next to the dock where

I was sitting. How she'd gotten out of her room remained a mystery. I thought of her eating pistachio ice cream and dancing cheek to cheek to jukebox music. She lived to be an old woman with no family, but she died too soon.

I put the ring back and took out Stella's postcard collection. Her daughter had taken a few cards and given me the rest. Despite a tiny figure bent from osteoporosis, Stella wasn't fragile. If she had any secret, it must only have been about loneliness. She'd stayed in a marriage with a husband who was often absent and raised a child she set free to travel. I'd remember her not as skinny and stooped but as Sturdy Stella.

I looked at the three other mementos. Lucy's sketchbook that I opened to a drawing of the boulder that held her name and the names of her friends. The ferns she'd drawn in front looked lush. I touched Jane's Jumble calendar that I'd finish as the year drew on and Barb's copy of Margaret Atwood's *Dearly* with the poem she'd written for me tucked inside.

I put aside my bag when I saw the boat returning. Only James was in it. I took my feet out of the water and waited for him to tie up. "Where's Richard?" I wanted to say goodbye to Heron Island with Richard, not James.

"He's right behind me. He borrowed a boat from the couple who own that old house on the lake. I remember it from when I was a kid. Jonathan and I used to sail by it, hoping to see the girl who hung out on the raft. Jonathan was planning to ask her on a date. He never got a chance."

"Your mother told me what happened. I'm sorry."

"It was a long time ago. Come to the house with me. My mother will want to be on the dock to say goodbye to you and Richard."

I slipped my feet into my sandals and walked with him. His breathing was labored. I hoped he didn't have a health problem. Dottie had seen enough deaths.

We found her in the living room, looking at the urn. She stood up when she heard us. "Promise me one thing, Nataki."

"Promise what?"

"That you'll mix some of my ashes in there with my friends."

"I promise," I said, wondering why she asked me, not James. Did she know something that she hadn't shared?

"No one will move that urn," said James. "I'll bring you here anytime you want to visit. You, too, Nataki."

"We'll come with my baby. We know she's a girl. We can watch her play on the beach and listen to her learn the names of birds. Dottie can tell her about all the women whose names are on the boulder, have her trace the letters and learn her alphabet."

"I'd like that," Dottie said as she went into the dining room. She picked up a potted fern that hadn't been there earlier. "When you and Richard find that house to buy, plant this. Can you keep it alive until then?"

"As alive as my memories of you all."

The sound of the boat approaching the dock filled the air. I struggled to keep from crying. "Come say goodbye on the dock."

We walked slowly out of the house toward the quiet water of Lake Winnipesaukee. The family of mallards was swimming around the dock. I could tell that Richard was anxious to leave. He was holding the rope so it wouldn't drift into the lake. He handed it to me while he hugged Dottie. "I'll be sure Nataki visits you. You'll be the first to know when our baby is born. We're naming her Dorothy."

"Dorothy Heron Anderson. In honor of all this year has taught us." I gave the rope back to Richard and clung to Dottie as if I wouldn't be seeing her again. I let her go and said to James, "Let me know when you get her settled into Sugar Hill. I'll be the first to visit."

I stepped into the boat and kept my body turned so I could wave to Dottie and James. When their figures became so small I could barely see them, I faced the front. I buried the guilt I felt for supplying the Mad Honey that killed Barb and Jane. An investigation had found one jar at the Wolfeboro Inn and I confessed that I'd destroyed another one. It was an accident. No one asked about a woman with dementia wandering into Lake Winnipesaukee, another one who tripped on the stairway, a third with a diabetic attack. Thelma and Stella and Lucy were old women.

I looked at Richard. Sun bounced off the scar on his temple. He was tanned and muscular and as handsome as the day we met. He'd never liked the job, never bonded with these women the way I had. If there were secrets to keep, I'd keep them and keep a marriage that would lead Richard and me into our nineties.

Six old women. Six lives with secrets and sorrows, joy and friendship and love.

I felt a kick inside me. Dorothy Heron Anderson. My baby. Our baby. The light of the sun sparkled on the water, beckoning us forward.

Shuffleboard

I COME EVERY DAY to the hospice facility where Brenda is dying of cancer. I'm her health care proxy, her only living relative, the one who consults with the nurses before I go into the room to see her. They tell me if she's been awake in the night, if she called out something in her sleep, if she asked for water, asked for me.

Today's nurse is my favorite. Milly. Short and chubby with breasts made for cuddling babies that neither Brenda nor I ever had despite the four marriages between us. Milly puts the roses I picked from Brenda's garden into a vase. Old-fashioned yellow roses that haven't had their smell hybridized out.

"She's been restless all afternoon, Gail," Milly says. "Talking nonsense about shuffleboard."

I look at Brenda, her body so light it seems to float on the bed the way she could float in the frigid water of Newfound Lake. She's a ghost of the girl who always beat me at shuffleboard, of the woman who spent her life running, in marathons and triathlons, on solitary backpacking trips, away from three marriages, from whatever secret has haunted her. I stroke her brow, her bald head that once was thick with blond hair.

"I'll just sit with her for a bit," I say. "I'll call you when I'm ready to leave."

Milly sets the vase of flowers onto the table next to Brenda's bed. As she leaves the room, she says, "It won't be long now."

I smelled the roses that hedge Woodard's property line behind the shuffleboard court. Brenda and I unbuttoned our shirts so when Paul arrived he'd see our bathing suits. Paul spent the entire summer at Woodard's where he stayed with his father in the cottage next to ours. He was eighteen last year, and we started to notice his good looks. Every morning Uncle Henry made us cover ourselves for shuffleboard. A couple of mornings ago, I heard him tell Aunt Fay, "I don't care if it's 1959. There are too many old men gawking at Brenda and Gail like they're fifteen-year-old Lolitas."

I shelved *Lolita* many times during my after-school job in the library. You had to be eighteen to check the book out, but I hid in the stacks and read it, a few pages at a time. I wasn't finished, but I had read far enough to know that Lolita was twelve, not fifteen, and that the old guy, Humphrey or Hubert or something like that, kept looking at her in a way he shouldn't. Old men might look at Brenda with her mature breasts and her thick blond hair that she wore in a flip curled just slightly at the edges. I wanted to tell Uncle Henry that no one would gawk at my untamable red curls, my face full of freckles, my barely noticeable breasts.

I positioned my shuffleboard cue on the black disc and pushed. It stopped at the 7 section.

"Gotcha already," Brenda called from the other end of the court. She pushed her disc and knocked my black one into the 10-Off area, leaving her yellow one safe in the 7 spot.

I pushed Brenda's disc onto the 8. It touched the line. She followed, leaving hers on the 10. Two more shots each and Brenda beat me again.

"Seventeen for me," said Brenda. "You start in the hole with 8 minus 10."

"Negative 2. I get it," I said. "You have a long way to 75. I'll catch up."

I didn't really think so. Brenda had been beating me every day for a week. No matter who won this game, we'd still take off the shirts we wore over our bathing suits, tie them around our waists, and walk past Paul on his lifeguard stand. We'd hold our cues over our shoulders like hunting rifles. He'd look down at us, maybe glimpsing a bit of cleavage. If I had cleavage.

Brenda was what every girl in school wanted to be, beautiful, athletic, funny. I rode her popularity because she let me. We weren't just cousins. We were best friends who shared our secrets. Or most of them. Brenda was the one who helped me choose glasses that didn't announce my bookishness. They made my eyes sparkle as much as the rhinestones embedded in the frames. She helped me find a bathing suit that had a little padding on the top, helped me cut off my dungarees so they fringed just below my butt. She chose the sleeveless shirts we wore to play shuffleboard and showed me how to tie mine to expose my midriff.

Four old men arrived at the shuffleboard court, waiting for us to finish our game. They were two of the teams from the shuffleboard tournament Uncle Henry used to play in. Now he never got out of bed until noon. Every day when we went back to the cottage for lunch, he'd be sitting in a rocking chair on the porch reading the paper, sipping from a tall glass of tomato juice. Aunt Fay would be in the kitchen fixing sandwiches. I wondered why she never came to the beach in the morning while Uncle Henry slept.

Brenda pushed her yellow disc onto the 7. "No points. It's touching the line," said one of the men from the sidelines. He was the man who played gin rummy with Uncle Henry after dinner while Aunt Fay went out. We never asked where. She'd tell us we should make sure the men behaved. We'd ignore them, go onto the porch, and plug in the new record player Brenda had gotten for Christmas. We'd listen to The Platters' "My Prayer" and Elvis's "Love Me Tender," over and over, imagining ourselves with Paul, while Uncle Henry and his friend got louder and louder.

Those nightly card games and Aunt Fay's disappearances began two vacations ago when Uncle Henry stopped playing games of Monopoly with us. He used to get himself a beer out of the refrigerator, make popcorn, hand cokes to Brenda and me and a glass of wine to Aunt Fay. Sometimes the game would last the entire two weeks of our vacation. I liked Monopoly better than blocking out Uncle Henry's gin rummy with music that was Brenda's choice. I never told her how much I hated The Platters.

"You winning again, Brenda?" said the gin rummy man.

"She's not winning yet," I said, pushing my last disc. It landed on the 10.

Brenda pushed the discs to the side of the court.

"75-68," I said to the man. "First time I've won this year. We'll return these so you can check them out in your names." I put the black discs into their carrying rack, picked it up with my left hand, almost four pounds of weight that challenged my arm muscle. I held the cue over my shoulder.

After Brenda packed up her discs, she stopped in front of Uncle Henry's friend. "Will you be playing cards tonight? What's the game called? Gin?" She walked past him without waiting for an answer, kicking angrily at the sand.

"You shouldn't be so upset," I said. "It's the first time I've beaten you all week."

She rested her arm on my shoulder, the cue she was carrying running parallel alongside mine. "I'm not angry with you. I don't like that guy."

"Why not? We never talk to him."

"Can't you hear him and my dad while they play cards? By the time Mom gets home, it's a yelling fest. My dad's the loudest. Just like at home."

"I never hear your dad yell. Well, maybe when we're on vacation, but that's because he's excited about the game."

"You must be deaf."

We reached the booth where we returned the shuffleboard equipment and signed ourselves out. Before we headed toward the shore and the lifeguard stand, we took off our shirts and put them into our bags. Brenda reached into her bag for a bottle of baby oil laced with iodine. "To the best tans on the beach," she said.

"Ones that Paul can't ignore," I said, knowing that I'd last a half hour before I'd have to cover up or my skin would burn to blisters. After a week at Woodard's, my face wore enough freckles for a new galaxy. While I added more freckles, Brenda would add another shade to her darkly tanned body. I wondered if we really shared some of the same genes or if one of us had been fathered by the mailman.

We found a spot close to the water and spread out our blanket. Brenda unscrewed the top of the baby oil. "We should swim first," I said. "Aren't you hot?"

"In more ways than one." Brenda screwed the cap back on and walked to the shoreline. She dove in without testing the water.

I inched my way slowly into the water, feeling its cold on my ankles, my shins, my knees. When I was in as high as my waist, I dove. As I pulled myself onto the raft,

Brenda was lying on her back, her eyes closed as if she were dreaming. She looked so much older this year. Paul called me Gail, but Brenda's was the name he always said first. I was an afterthought. I lay down next to Brenda, closing my eyes against the sun that warmed the goose bumps off my body.

Brenda rolled onto her elbow to face me. "Do you think Paul will come to the dance tonight?"

"Doesn't he have to?" I knew that Woodard's Fourth of July fireworks and dance were supposed to create some kind of bonding between the guests and the staff.

"He didn't come last year," Brenda said.

"I hardly remember it. Except that it was way too hot. I don't know how your mother danced so much with Paul's dad." I could still see Aunt Fay jitterbugging to "Blue Suede Shoes." She wore a black skirt that swept around her knees as Mr. Nolan led her through complicated turns under his arm, behind his back, the two of them side by side, breaking apart, facing each other in steps that moved them close, then away, until he crossed her arms over her head and pulled her backwards into a dip at the end of the songs.

I stopped thinking about last year and let the sun do its job, drying the cold water on my body, turning it into sweat. I sat up and watched the rhythm of the boats on the lake. A powerboat pulling a water-skier wove in and out of a line of three sailboats that must have come from the summer camp farther up the shore. I spun around so I could see Woodard's beach. Brenda pushed herself up so she was sitting beside me.

"Why doesn't your father dance?" I said. "Your mom is so good, I bet she could teach him."

"He'd rather sit on the porch with a book and a beer. Mr. Nolan will take care of my mother's dancing needs." She stood up. "It's too hot. I'm going to ask Paul if he's coming to the dance." She dove into the water and swam toward shore. Her crawl was perfect, much stronger than mine. She could have swum the width of Newfound Lake.

I hated to dive, so I used the ladder to lower myself off the raft. After the warm sun on my body, the water felt even colder. I twisted away from the raft and swam to shore. Close enough in, I stood. Brenda was in front of the lifeguard stand, her yellow two-piece bathing suit showing off her tight waist and her tanned skin. Paul was looking down, high enough above her that I was sure he could see the tops of her breasts. He was laughing. I glanced down at my own bathing suit top. Nothing showed above it but the freckles on my chest. I walked to our blanket, dodging two preschoolers who were carrying water in buckets, trying to fill a hole they had dug. The water seeped away as fast as they filled it. It reminded me of the myth of Sisyphus. Roll the rock up, roll it down, roll it up again. It was like Brenda and me. Best friends yesterday, rivals today, best friends again, I hoped, after this year's vacation where the only person who interested her was Paul.

I picked up my towel, dried myself off and, keeping it draped over my back to block off the sun, sat down on the blanket. I took my hat out of my bag. If I had to wear a hat, I wanted to wear this year's fashion. Its conical shape shaded my face, its straw putting yellow highlights onto my red hair.

Brenda came up behind me and sat on the blanket. "He's coming to the dance," she said, rubbing baby oil on her legs. "What should I wear?"

"Your red pedal pushers. I'll wear my navy blue ones." It wasn't like we'd packed a trunk full of clothes. Bathing suits, dungarees, last year's version cut off into shorts. We were going to sit in the sand to watch the fireworks then dance in Woodard's pavilion to music pumped through a loudspeaker by some local DJ we never heard of. Only the old people like Aunt Fay wore skirts they packed for the evenings they went out to dinner.

"Obviously," said Brenda. "What top? Not the ones we wear for shuffleboard. We don't want to look like twins."

"I packed my white one with the baby doll sleeves."

Brenda turned her head for a glance at Paul. "I'll wear my sleeveless one with the blue and white stripes."

Brenda's blouse was so tight fitting Uncle Henry had refused to pay for it. Aunt Fay let her keep it as long as Brenda didn't wear it to school. "You'll look like an American flag," I said.

"Better than a baby doll. You should wear your light blue one with the long sleeves. Hide your sunburn."

"Maybe," I threw off the towel, put on the blouse I'd worn for shuffleboard, and rolled onto my stomach. Brenda lay next to me. We stayed quiet until we heard the noon chimes that Woodard's used to signal that there would be no lifeguard on duty during the lunch hour.

Brenda jumped from our blanket and gathered her bag. "You can fold the blanket," she said.

By the time I stood up, she was at the lifeguard stand. Paul was on the sand next to her. They were laughing. I walked toward them in time to hear Paul say, "See you tonight," before he left.

"He's off duty this afternoon," Brenda said. "Maybe we should take naps so we'll be good for tonight."

"On the beach," I said. "After a game of shuffleboard." The shuffleboard court was always free after lunch. Old people's nap time, Brenda and I always said.

We crossed the street that separated Woodard's inn and beach from the hill where fifteen yellow cottages, brightened by red roofs, horseshoed the grass. I could see Aunt Fay standing on the porch talking with Mr. Nolan. He turned around, waved, and then went next door into his cottage. Uncle Henry was sitting in the rocking chair on our porch. He pulled Aunt Fay onto his lap, kissed her on the cheek. She pushed herself off him to go inside where she would prepare our lunch. I saw her rub the kiss off her cheek.

When we climbed the three steps to the porch, Uncle Henry slammed the book he was reading onto the table next to him, nearly knocking over his tomato juice. He looked up long enough to say, "You beat her again, Brenda?"

"I finally won," I said. "75-68."

"Well I'll be. Life does bring surprises." He grabbed his tomato juice and swallowed half of it.

Brenda and I went into the tiny kitchen area where Aunt

Fay had put fried bologna sandwiches on the table for us. I hated bologna, but I couldn't survive the afternoon with the pickle and handful of potato chips that lay beside it. I'd manage a few bites and hope Uncle Henry wouldn't come down to the beach. Brenda and I would go to the ice cream parlor where a sign said Woodard's chocolate was the best in New England. I didn't know if that was true, but its chocolate ice cream was my favorite from anywhere.

Uncle Henry didn't come inside for lunch. When Brenda asked if he was coming to the beach, I knew she was also thinking about the ice cream parlor. She didn't like bologna any more than I did.

"Your dad's not feeling well," said Aunt Fay, who was standing at the counter eating her sandwich and chopping vegetables for some kind of interesting salad we'd have for supper. She was good at salads. She laced them with chicken or tuna or eggs or, on occasion, with salami or a kind of ham whose name I couldn't pronounce. Procudo or something. We'd have bread from Woodard's bakery and it would be better than the Wonder Bread that sandwiched our bologna. At least we wouldn't have Spam and pineapple tonight.

"He'll rest up for the fireworks," said Aunt Fay.

"Do you think he'll stay for the dance this year?" I said, forcing down a bit of bologna.

"He doesn't dance," said Brenda. She kicked me under the table.

"I hope he doesn't have something contagious," I said. "My stomach's a little funny. I'm sorry, Aunt Fay, but I can't finish my sandwich." I'd buy a large ice cream cone. Uncle Henry might care about how many calories Brenda and I consumed, but I didn't. "Bony Moronie," our friends had started calling me after the song came out.

"Maybe you should stay in the cottage this afternoon," said Aunt Fay. "Get better for the fireworks."

"She'll be fine," said Brenda, kicking me under the table again. "We're going to nap on the beach."

"I'll be down around two o'clock," said Aunt Fay. "I need a good long swim."

Aunt Fay loved to swim in the cold water of Newfound Lake as much as Brenda did. Every afternoon she'd swim way out beyond the raft and do laps for an hour or more. She'd come back on shore, her skin glowing red, her face relaxed. She'd say the same thing every day, "I love this lake. It's so clear I can count the boulders the glaciers left under the water thousands of years ago." After her geology lesson, Aunt Fay would sit on one of the Adirondack chairs that stood in a line along the beach, their colors the same yellow and red as the cottages. She'd read until just before dinner when she'd have another, shorter swim.

Until last year, Uncle Henry would play a game of shuffleboard, swim to the raft, and lie there until Brenda and I swam out to join him. He'd play king of the raft, not letting Brenda and me climb on. When he gave up pushing us away, we'd get on. It took all our strength to push him off. He'd turn onto his back, give us a salute, then swim to shore where he'd sit next to Aunt Fay. Sometimes when Brenda and I left the raft, we'd also sit on the chairs, four people reading, happy together. I missed the way Uncle Henry used to be.

We finished our lunch, covered ourselves with the shirts we'd taken off against the heat of the cottage. I checked the pocket of my shorts to be sure I still had the money I stuffed inside when I put them on over my bathing suit in the morning.

Aunt Fay smiled as she picked up my half-eaten sandwich. "Maybe the ice cream will settle your stomach." She shooed us out the door, past Uncle Henry who had finished his tomato juice and was drinking a beer Aunt Fay had brought him with his sandwich.

The afternoon dragged. Brenda beat me at shuffleboard again. My ice cream cone dripped on my bathing suit and didn't rinse off when we swam to the raft. We stayed on it so long the sun burned my back enough that I'd get a post-burn chill at the dance. In a few days, I'd be peeling off dead skin.

Paul's dad came to the beach, but Paul never appeared. Uncle Henry surprised us by coming to the shuffleboard court to play with his gin rummy friend. He kept looking over at Aunt Fay, who sat on a chair next to Mr. Nolan. We got bored with the beach and told her we were going for a walk. If Uncle Henry's game was finished when we got back, we'd play shuffleboard again. We'd be back at the cottage in time for dinner.

We walked along the road that ran next to summer houses lining the lake. Rich people's houses, we called them. They had verandas overlooking the lake, sandy beaches, and grass mowed smooth enough for croquet. When the road curved with the lake at the summer camp, we saw Paul on the camp's tennis court softly hitting balls to a group of ten year olds.

"He works there two afternoons a week," said Brenda. "He's good with kids."

"You know a lot about him," I said.

"He told me this morning while you were taking your time getting off the raft."

Paul didn't see us. Before we turned around, Brenda yelled, "I'll see you at the dance."

He waved and went back to lobbing tennis balls to the campers. We walked slowly to the beach where I managed to beat Brenda at shuffleboard for the second time that day.

"I wasn't concentrating," she said.

"Dreaming about Paul," I said as we walked toward the cottage and dinner.

"And other things."

Uncle Henry was already at the table buttering his bread when we came into the kitchen. "About time, girls," he said, continuing to eat.

Aunt Fay motioned us to the chairs. "Eat now, then you can get ready for the fireworks." She sat down next to Uncle Henry and scooped salad onto her plate before she passed the bowl to Brenda.

"Will you come to the fireworks and dance tonight?" I asked Uncle Henry.

"Fireworks. I'll leave your aunt to Bill Nolan after that." He chugged his beer.

Aunt Fay put down the fork she had halfway to her mouth. She pushed aside her chair and went out to the porch. When she came back and sat down, I could see that she was angry. Uncle Henry didn't like Mr. Nolan, maybe because he was Paul's father. He wasn't blind. He knew Brenda and I liked Paul. He thought we were still too young for boys.

We finished eating, dressed for the fireworks, and killed time waiting for them by playing a game of Scrabble with Aunt Fay. Uncle Henry sat on the porch reading a book and drinking beer.

At 8:30 the four of us walked to the beach. Mr. Nolan was on his porch smoking a cigarette.

"Paul's down on the beach," he called out to us. "I'll be watching from here. I hate the noise of fireworks. See you at the dance, girls."

"Guess I'm chopped liver," said Uncle Henry.

"That's enough, Henry," said my aunt. "Bill knows you hate to dance."

At the bottom of the slope, we crossed the road to the inn, which was framed against a sky made pink by the reflection of the sun setting behind the cabins. The humidity of the day had lifted, but the night would still be warm.

On the beach, we passed a group of children twirling sparklers, and running aimlessly on the sand. Aunt Fay spread a blanket next to the shuffleboard court. Uncle Henry looked around for a vacant Adirondack chair. "I told you we should have come earlier," he said. "I'm going back. Sit on the porch like Bill Nolan."

"Suit yourself," said Aunt Fay.

"That son of his is on the lifeguard stand. Don't flirt too much, girls." Uncle Henry pronounced "girls" in a voice that mimicked Mr. Nolan's. He stooped to squeeze Aunt Fay's shoulder. "You either, Fay." She didn't answer as he walked away from us.

Brenda sat on the sand beside the blanket, leaning over so she could nestle against her mother's thigh. I was on the opposite side of the blanket, my knees bent up against my chest, my arms wrapped around them in the kind of fetal position I often used. Brenda always teased me about it, saying I was the only person she knew who could return to the womb.

A rowboat with three men in it pushed off the shore. Two of the men got onto the raft. The third lifted a box to them, then rowed away from the raft farther into the lake. The fireworks began in an explosion of sound. Bursts of light followed, as small and bright as the sparklers the kids had been twirling. The momentum of the display increased. Balls broke into every color of the rainbow, each one faster and bigger and more spectacular than the last until a pause before the finale. Seconds passed, then a blast shot a rocket into the air followed by another and another and another in quick succession. Shards of light roared into the sky, broke apart into a kaleidoscope of shapes and colors that merged with the stars. From the pavilion, a Sousa march announced the end of the fireworks. Whenever I heard it, I thought of the Girl Scout song about being kind to our web-footed friends.

"Fireworks are better every year," said Aunt Fay.

"Let's dance," said Brenda when the march turned to Jerry Lee Lewis singing "Great Balls of Fire."

The pavilion was nothing more than a roof and a wooden floor held up by pillars that left it open on all sides. Tonight its roof was lined with red, white, and blue lights. An American flag flew on a pole just outside the pavilion. Forty-eight stars, but after today Alaska would be a state and the flag would have forty-nine. An odd number to try to arrange until a fiftieth would be added for Hawaii in a year. Aunt Fay liked to say that the flag's stars would grow up with Brenda and me.

When we stepped into the pavilion, we saw Paul talking with the disc jockey, who spun records from a corner. The DJ nodded. "Great Balls of Fire" ended, replaced with the slow chords of "Love Me Tender." Paul walked over to us, put his hand out to Brenda, and pulled her onto the dance floor. I stood on the sidelines watching, a wallflower waiting to be picked.

Aunt Fay stood next to me. "Your time will come," she said. She scanned the people as they gathered in the pavilion.

"Where is Paul's dad?" I asked. "You're both great dancers."

"I don't know. He should be here." She accepted the hand of one of the men I recognized from the shuffleboard teams this morning. They caught the last few bars of "Love Me Tender" and stayed on the dance floor jitterbugging to "Party Doll." The man didn't dance nearly as well as Mr.

Nolan. I stopped paying attention when a boy whose name I didn't know asked me to dance. I was surprised at how good he was, pleased that we looked better on the dance floor than Paul and Brenda.

After "Party Doll," the DJ put on "Young Love." Apparently my partner didn't slow dance because he left me in the middle of the floor. He went outside the pavilion where I saw him light a cigarette. Brenda and Paul stayed on the floor, her head on his shoulder, his hand resting on her bottom. Aunt Fay was still dancing with the shuffleboard man. She broke away to say something to Paul, who shrugged and continued dancing. His father had still not arrived.

The music turned fast again and I danced with a new partner. The DJ's rhythm continued to vary between slow and fast. I danced several more times, even slow dances, with the boy whose name I still didn't know. We got noticed on the floor and I became almost popular, dancing with half-a-dozen other boys. Brenda and Paul never broke apart. When the DJ announced an intermission, Aunt Fay said she was tired, she was going back to the cottage. I carried a glass of punch outside and saw her walking along the road, away from the cottages. I guessed that she didn't want to go home to Uncle Henry, who'd be complaining about the noise of the music.

I sat alone, drinking my punch, wondering why Mr. Nolan hadn't come to the dance. The post sunburn chill I expected arrived. As soon as the break was over, I needed to dance it away. A couple came outside and walked hand in hand to the edge of the stand where we rented the shuffleboard equipment. Brenda and Paul. They kissed then separated, Paul walking away and along the side of the inn toward the cottages. Brenda disappeared around the side of the rental stand. After several minutes, she reappeared and walked toward me.

"What's wrong?" I said. "Why did Paul leave?"

"He's looking for his father."

"So's your mother."

"Why do you say that?" Brenda was digging her sneakers into the sand.

"She left. I saw her walking down the road instead of to our cottage. I think she missed dancing with Paul's dad."

"I'm sure she did. Don't know why she'd think he was down the road."

Neither did I, but I guessed he was not at his cottage, or ours, drinking beer with Uncle Henry.

The music started again. Brenda took off her sneakers, emptying out the sand and putting them on again. "Let's go in. We might as well keep dancing."

This time it was Brenda who was the wallflower. Maybe boys, even grown men, were afraid of her. After three songs with no one asking her to dance, she left, telling me she'd see me back at the cottage. The dance was almost over anyway. I started to follow her, but got pulled onto the floor by the boy without a name. We stayed together for the rest of the night, even slow dancing to the last song, "Moments to Remember."

When he asked to walk me back to our cottage, I

said okay. He reached for my hand as we walked up the middle path to the top of the horseshoe. "What's your name?" he said.

"Gail. What's yours"" I wasn't sure I liked holding hands, but I didn't know how to get out of it.

"Marty." In front of the cottage, he bent to kiss me. I backed away. "Okay, then," he said and left me standing alone in the dark.

Brenda came out of the cottage and sat on the edge of the porch, her feet on the one step that elevated it from the ground.

"Why'd you leave?" I asked.

"No point in staying. Paul's gone to bed."

"Is your mother home?" I said. "Did she find his dad?"

"How should I know? If she did, they got back here before me. My mother's sleeping. So's my father."

I looked at Paul's cabin. His father sat hunched in a chair. He looked like he was sleeping, too. "Let's go to bed. Shuffleboard in the morning. My turn for the yellow discs."

We got into our pajamas and into bed quietly so we wouldn't wake Aunt Fay and Uncle Henry. I woke sometime in the night to the sound of rain. I thought I heard footsteps but ignored them. I didn't want to know who was outside in the middle of a rainy night. Nothing stirred in our cabin, not even Uncle Henry snoring.

It had stopped raining when we woke to a siren and voices of people running up the path. I pulled a sweatshirt over my pajamas and went outside. Mr. Nolan was on his porch in the same position as last night. Paul was standing beside him. He ignored my wave. Below on the road, a police car was parked, its blue lights flashing, an ambulance parked behind it. I watched two men carry a stretcher onto the Nolans' porch. Two policemen led Paul into the cottage.

Aunt Fay and Uncle Henry came up behind me. "I'm going over there," said Aunt Fay.

Uncle Henry caught her arm. "Stay here. There's nothing we can do."

"What's happening?" said Brenda, coming onto the porch in her baby doll pajamas. "Where's Paul?"

Before anyone could answer, the policemen came out of the cottage and led Paul down the path to the cruiser. The other two men picked up Mr. Nolan from his chair and put him on a stretcher. They covered him and carried him to the ambulance.

"He must have had a heart attack," said Uncle Henry. He put his arms around Aunt Fay and Brenda. "We can't do anything now. Make breakfast, Fay."

"How can any of us eat?" said Aunt Fay.

"We can try. We'll learn more later."

When later came, we were sitting on the porch. Crime scene tape had appeared around the cottage, so we knew it wasn't a heart attack. Two police officers came to our cottage. They sent Aunt Fay onto the porch. She sat on the step staring, her back toward us.

I strained to hear what Uncle Henry was saying. "… home right after the fireworks… heard nothing… never saw Bill."

One of the police officers brought Uncle Henry onto the porch and called in Aunt Fay.

"Did someone kill Mr. Nolan?" I asked Uncle Henry.

"Appears so," he said.

Brenda walked off the porch and down the hill to the water. I followed her. When I caught up, she was in front of the lifeguard stand crying. She pushed me away.

As I walked back up the hill, I stopped the police officers who were going into another cottage. "Are you talking to everyone?" I said.

One of them looked down on me as if I were ten years old. "All the adults," he said.

"I heard someone outside in the middle of the night," I said.

"That would be about right." He didn't care to ask me anything else.

I went onto our porch. Inside I could hear Uncle Henry and Aunt Fay. "I left the dance alone," said Aunt Fay. "I never found him."

"It's over, then," said Uncle Henry.

I went into the cottage and asked, "What's over?"

"Don't eavesdrop," said Uncle Henry. He went outside, slamming the door behind him.

Aunt Fay looked like she'd been crying. "Brenda's crying, too," I said. "What happened to Paul?"

"They're taking him to his mother. She lives in Maine."

"Did he kill his father?"

"Of course not. Go find Brenda. Tell her he'll be fine. Tell her to come back here. We need to be together."

I left Aunt Fay alone. Outside I saw Uncle Henry walking along the road. I went to the beach where Brenda was still sitting on the sand, now digging a hole with a toy shovel some child had forgotten. I thought of the kids and their water hole. Her digging was just as futile. I told her about Paul. She said nothing and kept digging until I put my hand on hers. She pushed it off and stood up. "I need to do something," she said.

"Your mother says we should go back to the cottage."

"Not yet," she said. "I don't want to see my dad."

"He's not there."

"He will be."

I wondered why Brenda wanted to stay away from her dad, but I didn't ask. "How about shuffleboard? No one's around. No one's going to do anything today."

We went to the rental stand, which was never locked. When we picked up the carriers, we saw that one of the yellow discs was missing, so we went back to the cottage. Uncle Henry and Aunt Fay were sitting at the kitchen table. Aunt Fay had been crying and Uncle Henry hadn't shaved. I could smell beer he'd spilled on his shirt. They didn't argue when we asked for money. We said we'd have ice cream for lunch. We spent the rest of the day swimming and reading on the beach.

After dinner, Uncle Henry still hadn't shaved, but the smell of beer was gone. He told us we were leaving in the morning. Rain was coming in and Aunt Fay didn't want to be shut inside thinking of Mr. Nolan. We went to bed early. Brenda and I listened to Uncle Henry telling Aunt

Fay something about Bill and a shuffleboard disc.

"Someone hit Mr. Nolan with the yellow shuffleboard disc," I whispered to Brenda.

She turned onto her stomach and said nothing else for the rest of the night.

We woke to an empty cottage, a note on the table saying that Aunt Fay and Uncle Henry were walking. I fixed myself a bowl of cereal and ate on the porch. I could hear Brenda moving through the cottage. She was an obsessive packer, always checking every room for a lost sock or a pair of underpants that hadn't made it to the laundry basket. She came outside wearing a bathing suit under a sweatshirt and carrying a towel.

"It's freezing," I said. "You aren't going swimming?"

"My last time. We'll never come back to Newfound Lake." She left, clutching the towel as if it were protecting her.

When Brenda returned, Uncle Henry stopped her on the porch and said, "Find anything you left behind?"

"Nothing you need," she said, dripping water from her wet bathing suit onto the floor Aunt Fay had just cleaned.

"You're crazy, Brenda," said Aunt Fay. "It's too cold to swim."

"It's okay now," Brenda said.

An hour later, the rain arrived. We hauled our things to Uncle Henry's car in the parking lot, plastic bags that grocery stores had just started to sell draped over boxes and suitcases to keep them dry. Brenda was right. We never again vacationed at Woodard's. The next year, she told me she'd had a letter from Paul saying that he was living with his mother in Maine. He was sorry he'd no longer lifeguard at Woodard's. We never learned who might have killed Mr. Nolan. If I suggested the gin rummy man or one of the shuffleboard men, Brenda ignored me. For the rest of our lives, she refused to talk about that vacation.

After that summer, Uncle Henry and Aunt Fay began to spend Fourth of July week on Cape Cod. Until I finished college, I vacationed with them. Uncle Henry had no one to play gin rummy with, so we played Scrabble in the evening. He'd drink one beer and Aunt Fay would have her glass of wine. If I mentioned Woodard's, they'd talk about the ice cream parlor, the water that was colder than Cape Cod's, and the cottages arranged like a horseshoe on the hill. Brenda never said anything. It was years before I understood that Uncle Henry had been drinking those last two summers at Woodard's. Brenda never spoke about it and I never asked.

Brenda went out of state to college and drifted through a variety of jobs in whatever city a current boyfriend or husband brought her to. Only after her parents died and she had left a third husband, did she come back to New Hampshire for good. The year she returned, I suggested that we take a vacation on Newfound Lake. She wouldn't go back to Newfound, so we went to Winnipesaukee instead. She swam as powerfully as she always had. Though we were well into our fifties, she wore a bikini on a body as toned as a teenager's. She would lie on the raft or on the beach sunbathing while I lathered myself with sunscreen and wore a shirt over my one-piece bathing suit. When I said that the lifeguard looked a little like Paul Nolan, she dug her feet in the sand.

"The past is dead and gone," she said. "Just like my parents. Just like those cottages. I never think of them."

I wanted to ask what she meant by "them," but I knew she'd walk away as she always did if I mentioned Paul. The inn on Winnipesaukee had a shuffleboard court, but when Brenda wouldn't play, I began to wonder if she thought Paul had killed his father. I thought about our lives. They were like a game of shuffleboard. Sometimes the discs touched, sometimes they didn't come close, and sometimes they pushed another one away. Our relationship was like a shuffleboard set with one of the discs missing, a hole left that haunted us both.

I sit in what I think of as my vigil chair. I move Brenda's hand from under the blanket and hold it in my own. Brenda opens her eyes, turns her head to see the yellow roses.

"Shuffleboard," she says. I feel a slight squeeze of her hand. Her mouth opens and closes. She's trying to say something.

"Yellow… in the water," she says.

I pull my head back. "The yellow disc?"

She nods.

I remember her swim that last cold morning. "You had the disc? Threw it into the lake?"

She nods again.

"Paul gave it to you? He killed his father?" I bend to her ear.

"No. My father. In his suitcase."

A gag rises in her throat. Her hand drops from mine. She's won the last game of shuffleboard.

Hardscrabble

THE BETHLEHEM SERVICE Station wasn't the one Monica remembered from twenty years ago. No Eddie waddled out to pump her gas, wash her car window, ask about her widowed mother. No Eddie to babble about the difficulty of handling the gas taxes, the new restrictions at the town dump, and the guidelines for disposing of motor oil. Eddie's personality had been carved in the granite of The Granite State and like The Old Man of the Mountain, he had fallen after Monica moved away. Whoever owned the station now had turned the repair shop into a convenience store and the pumps into self-service.

Monica unscrewed her gas cap, swiped her credit card, and began to fill her tank. She wasn't anxious for her paragliding trip to end, but she'd be glad to get back to Oregon where every gas station had an Eddie to do the pumping for her. She and Charles had planned to fly in all thirty-nine states that had launch sites. He lasted through thirty-five before he said he was tired of sleeping in cheap hotels, tired of her dictating when and where they would launch, where and what they would eat. She said good riddance and finished the trip alone. She'd celebrate her last flight, splurging for a stay in the luxury of The Bethlehem Inn.

A silver SUV, dented on one side, pulled up to the pump beside her. She watched a pair of sneakers step onto the ground, her eyes moving up the man's jeans and flannel shirt, stopping at his face. In his forties, she guessed, with graying hair, a beard, and black-framed glasses. A little heavy-set for her taste, but not bad looking.

The man studied her as he swiped his credit card. "Oregon license plate. You're a long way from home."

She set the nozzle back onto the gas pump. "Used to live here. Twenty years ago."

"A long time. Visiting or coming home to stay?"

She wasn't back to stay and didn't know if she'd visit Aunt Gwen, so she said, "Neither. I'm here for the paragliding."

He squinted into the sun that was low on the horizon and adjusted his glasses. "Launching from Morningside?"

"Cannon. You know about paragliding?" She'd been flying alone since Charles left. Maybe she'd be lucky and this guy would join her. A last fling before returning to the routine of her life in Oregon.

"Not me. I know someone who flies. Tries to convince me, but I tell him I'd end up crashing into a tree. He tells me that Cannon's a difficult launch." He thrust the gas nozzle into his tank, turning his gaze from her to the meter.

She waited for him to speak again. When he didn't, she got into her car and drove away.

She stood in front of the sliding door she had cracked open to feel the chill of October in New Hampshire. Outside, the maples and oaks rose in reds and oranges mottled with the sun. She pushed back her wave of nostalgia, and opening the door wider, stepped onto the balcony. The morning songs of birds she never heard from her condo in Oregon filled the air. The water of the Ammonoosuc River flowed below the balcony.

She took her phone out of her bathrobe pocket and punched in the security code. Aunt Gwen's number ran through her head. 251-4153. How many times had she called Gwen's daughter before Jenny crashed into a tree while skiing an icy trail on Cannon? Monica had tried to speak to her in the hospital, but Jenny couldn't hear. Three days later, she died.

Cannon was a risky launch site, but Monica needed to fly over the mountain that had claimed her cousin's life that icy cold day they were skiing with Film. Quick, wiry Film, who in elementary school was so obsessed with the Olympian Phil Mahre that Monica called him Phil-M, a nickname that soon morphed into Film. In high school, he was the riskiest skier on the mountain and as handsome as a movie star. He was going to become an Olympian, then star in a remake of *Downhill Racer.*

She shook off the image of Jenny falling on Upper

Hardscrabble. Touching the keypad on her phone, she added the 603 area code. She half-hoped that Aunt Gwen wouldn't answer. But answer Gwen did, the same as always, saying "This is Gwen," as if the caller were expecting someone else.

Monica waited long enough that Gwen said, "Who's this?"

"It's Monica."

"Monica? Where are you? What do you need?"

Typical that Aunt Gwen would think she needed something.

"I don't need anything. I'm paragliding. Launching in a few hours."

"Launching?"

"Just the word we use to describe how we get our wings in the air to fly."

"Are you talking about those parachute things I see sometimes?"

"An elongated parachute. Like a wing."

"I've seen them. Pretty, but they look dangerous."

"Paragliding's no more dangerous than skiing," Monica said into the phone.

"That was cruel." When Monica didn't answer, Gwen continued, "Is Sierra with you? Don't know why you'd name a child for a mountain."

Monica was tempted to say it was a better name than Cannon. "It's a mountain range, not a mountain. She's with her father."

"So you married him?"

Monica wanted to scream, "Too many questions." She hadn't married Bryce. Said Sierra could live with him, he was a better mother than she was.

"Well?" Aunt Gwen was waiting for an answer about marrying Sierra's father.

"Never did. Bryce was a bad mate, but he's a good father."

"Your mother liked him," said Gwen. "The one time she visited."

Monica heard the criticism in Aunt Gwen's voice under the New Hampshire accent she'd forgotten was so strong. "I need to go," she said. "Catch the wind while I can."

"Who are you—what's the word—flying with?"

"I'm alone," said Monica.

"Did you just arrive? Where were you last night?"

So many questions annoyed her. "I'm at The Bethlehem Inn."

"Why aren't you staying here?"

Monica imagined how that would go. Questions. Criticism. A litany about Jenny that would remind her of how much she missed the cousin who was her best friend until they both became interested in Film. "I got in late. You were probably in bed," she lied.

"Are you staying longer? You can stay here."

"Just one more night. I'm all settled in. I'll stop by when I finish my flight."

"Shall I fix dinner? Lasagna?"

Monica could taste the lasagna that was Aunt Gwen's specialty. Maybe a visit would be worth it.

"Film was here last night," said Aunt Gwen.

The name startled Monica. "He's still around? I haven't seen him since Jenny died and I left for college."

She could hear Aunt Gwen suck in her breath before she said, "It was hard on him. He stopped skiing."

"I heard he went to Colorado to train with Phil Mahre, try for the '92 Olympics."

"He lost his edge. Came back after you left for Oregon. Got a job as an EMT, but it didn't last. He couldn't stand the sight of the injured. Started drinking."

Monica wasn't surprised. Even in high school, Film celebrated with vodka after a ski race. Claimed it was water.

"Why does he visit you?"

"To talk about Jenny. He loved her you know. Blames you."

"Blames me for what?"

"Leaving Jenny on the mountain."

"It wasn't my fault she skied into that tree."

Aunt Gwen's voice cracked. "Film's mostly pulled himself together. Gets drunk sometimes and comes to talk about Jenny."

"Like last night?"

"Something set him off. It doesn't happen often. Anymore."

Monica didn't want to hear about someone whose glory days ended with high school. She didn't want to talk about Jenny. Still, she said, "I'll see you around six."

She pressed the red end call button and came back

into the room to dress in a tank top, wicking shirt, tights and jeans. Her fleece and puff jacket were draped across a chair, the jacket orange for easy visibility, though in New Hampshire's fall, that color choice wouldn't help. She put on wool socks and stepped into the sneakers that she'd exchange for hiking boots after breakfast. Everything else she needed was stuffed into her paragliding backpack. Her wing and all her equipment had worked well through thirty-eight states. Helmet, gloves, hydration pack, GPS navigator, miniature radio, all the highest lightweight quality to keep her pack under thirty pounds. She figured she had spent $10,000 since she tried that first lesson with Charles. The equipment had worn better than he did. She brushed her teeth and pulled her hair into a ponytail. She glanced in the mirror, telling herself that she could still pass for thirty. Not that anyone would care. Paraglider pilots watched the sky, not the people on the ground.

She stepped into the hallway, locked her door with the real key The Bethlehem Inn still used, and found her way downstairs to the breakfast room. It hadn't changed since she and Sierra had stayed there for her mother's funeral. At five, Sierra was full of questions about the olden days. Monica kept explaining that neither she nor Sierra's grandmother had been alive in 1867 when the inn was built. Sierra loved the wavy glass in the windows, the way the nails sank into the wood floors, the plaster on the walls, the stairs that creaked from ghosts walking. She announced that she wanted to stay in New Hampshire and live with her aunt. Gwen had embraced Sierra the way she had embraced Monica when she was Jenny's best friend.

The smell of coffee, bacon, and home-baked bread filled the breakfast room. A few couples and a family with three children sat at tables covered with tablecloths designed in a pattern of fall leaves. The Bethlehem Inn was a little worn around the edges, but it maintained a tradition of serving full breakfasts to order. Monica chose a table overlooking the river.

She studied the menu for a long time before a waiter finally appeared. Tall and too skinny, he looked hungover, red around the eyes, with the tired voice of someone who wasn't fully awake. "Ready to order?" he said.

"Eggs Benedict."

He wrote it down and started to leave the table. "With orange juice. And coffee right away," Monica said.

"Comes with the breakfast," he said, and walked away.

When he returned with a coffee pot, she held her cup toward him. He splashed some onto her hand, put the pot down, and took one of the napkins off the table. "Sorry," he said, fumbling to wipe her hand.

She cringed and pulled it away. "I'll do it."

"Whatever," he said. He walked to a table on the other side of the dining room. Something in the way he moved made Monica wonder if he was someone she knew in high school.

What the waiter lacked in finesse, the Eggs Benedict made up for. Eggs not too runny or hard, ham not too salty, hollandaise sauce the real thing. Monica fueled herself for her flight by eating every crumb. The waiter left the bill without speaking. Monica signed it, adding a grudging 10% tip.

Inside her room, she did a weather search on her phone. The forecast looked good, NNE winds 10 to 15 mph, and the lapse rate looked promising for getting to 6,000 feet. Cannon might be a difficult launch, but this looked like a crazy good day until a weather system was forecasted to approach around three o'clock. If she got off by noon, she could circle around the White Mountains for a couple of hours. She'd land at the recommended zone in Franconia. Someone there would drive her back to her car at Cannon. Paragliders supported each other.

The lot at Cannon was almost full when Monica turned into it. The whole of Franconia Notch was crowded with leaf peepers, tourists the locals hated even more than summer hikers and winter skiers. They drove too slowly and watched the scenery more than the roads. She wondered if they drove on Route 93 any more safely now that The Old Man of the Mountain had fallen. She was living with Bryce when they heard the news. He laughed and said, "That's geology."

She parked and took her key out of the ignition, an image of The Old Man dangling from her keychain with New Hampshire's state motto printed in tiny letters around it. "Live Free or Die." She was taking her backpack out of the trunk when a man got out of an SUV parked in the row in front of her. She recognized the dented car and the man from the gas station. He walked toward her. "Hi again," he said, looking at her pack. "Paragliding alone?"

"I am."

He held out a hand for her to shake. "I'm Mark."

"Monica. Are you hiking?"

"Lafayette."

"Nice trail. But long." She looked at his boots. New.

He saw her gaze and said, "A good way to break in my boots. Maybe we can meet later. Have a drink, dinner?"

"I'd like that," she said. A drink and a dinner sounded better than another tense conversation with Aunt Gwen about Jenny. She'd call her from the tram line and make an excuse.

He took his phone out of a shirt pocket. "You can't always control where you land. Call me and I'll pick you up."

She slammed the trunk of her car and reached into her backpack for her phone. She added the number he gave her, labeled the contact Mark, and gave him her number.

"Later, then," he said. "Unless you crash into a tree on top of the mountain."

She flinched, shrugged off the comment, and walked toward the tram, calling over her shoulder, "I'll contact you when I've landed. In one piece."

She stopped outside the entrance to the tram to call Aunt Gwen. A machine announced a polite, generic, "This is Gwen. Please leave a message."

"It's Monica. Something's come up. I need to cancel tonight. I'll call in the morning and we can have breakfast." By morning she'd have thought up an excuse for canceling dinner.

Inside the tram building, she paid the $25 fee and cursed the line waiting for the next car to come down the mountain. Worse than winter. At least then it wasn't filled with children asking, "What if the tram falls down?" "Why do the trees turn red?" "Is there food on top of the mountain?" When the only child in the tram said, "Are we going as high as God?" she tried to block out her voice and imagine herself rising in a thermal above the mountains.

She watched the tram approach, followed the line into it, and found a corner where she could set down her pack. She turned her back to the other passengers and looked out the side window facing away from Upper and Middle Hardscrabble. Below she saw the cuts of DJ's Tramline and Kinsman Glade that would soon be covered in snow.

The tram hit its landing platform, never a smooth stop. After the main crush of passengers exited, she lifted her pack, stepped onto the platform, and followed the child who had asked about God into the sunshine. She found the ridge where she'd launch and set her pack down next to a couple who had spread out their wings.

"I'm Elise," said the woman. "This is Phil." Monica shivered at the name.

"Good day for flying," said Phil, looking closely at her. "At least until that storm system gets close."

"Seems like," said Monica.

"I thought we knew all the pilots in New Hampshire," said Phil. "You new to the area?"

"Grew up here," said Monica. "First time back."

"Cannon's tricky. You flying alone?" said Phil.

"I am."

"Want our radio frequency?" he asked as he was clipping his radio onto his harness. "Just in case you need a contact."

"Thanks," said Monica. She accepted the offer even though she'd been risking flights with no contact since Charles left. She found her radio in her backpack and put in the frequency that Phil read out, 449.875.

"Have a good flight," said Elise. She ran backwards a few steps, let her wing fill and arch over her head, then turned toward to the slope, leaned, took a couple of steps and rose into the air. Phil launched a minute later. Their wings floated close together, neon green and yellow against the sky.

She unzipped her pack, pulled out the puff jacket she'd wear over her fleece, and put it on. Indian Summer was stingy at the top of Cannon Mountain. She took her wing out of the harness, laid it on the ground in front her, then checked that none of the lines were tangled. She rolled up her backpack and stuffed it into the storage compartment of the harness. Hydration pack, reserve parachute, radio, all okay. The batteries of the GPS navigator were low, but her flight wouldn't be long and she could easily see the landing zone in Franconia. All she wanted from the day was to fly over the mountains she had been away from too long.

She put on her helmet, sunglasses, and gloves, then

pulled the harness straps tight. She did her last safety check. Leg straps and chest strap good, carabiners locked, the GPS in her flight deck, boots tied. High in the distant sky, she could see the neon wings of the couple who had just launched.

She waited a few minutes, feeling the rhythm of the wind. When the cycle was good, she faced the wing and pulled the risers to inflate it. She felt a tug backwards, then a slow release as the wing arched over her head. She turned forward toward the valley, took a couple of steps until her wing caught and floated into the air. The wind carried her forward, smooth enough that she relaxed in her harness. Below, she saw trails she recognized cut into the mountain. She looked away from the Hardscrabbles and drifted over Profile Lake, Mittersill, Lafayette, Route 93 that narrowed as it wove through Franconia Notch. She imagined Mark hiking on Lafayette. If their meeting went well, she might stay a third night before she returned to Oregon and Sierra. Every time they talked on the phone, Sierra had another complaint. Some teacher or other was assigning homework the weekend of the semi-formal, Bryce wouldn't pay for the dress she wanted, Chelsea was trying to steal her boyfriend, on and on in a litany Monica remembered as her own.

She stopped thinking, letting the wing carry her high above the mountain. Hiking trails that snaked through the colors of fall along the ridges and the granite of rockier peaks lulled her. Images of Sierra morphed into a memory of hiking with Jenny on the Falling Waters trail.

She shook it away and breathed into a meditative state.

She floated, lost in time and the soft rush of the wind until the squawk of her radio startled her. A voice said, "This is Phil. We just landed. It's not even two o'clock, but the weather's already turning. Better get yourself down. Call and I'll pick you up."

"Will do," Monica said. A cloud bank was visible on the horizon. She knew she should land, but the conditions had been so perfect that she delayed. When she felt the first hint of turbulence, she searched for the landing site below. She had drifted too long. The air became choppy enough that she knew she couldn't wait to find the site. She checked her GPS. 2 mph, but she couldn't tell if that was forward or backward. With no place to land underneath her and no forward penetration, she had to turn and run with the wind. She tried to read the terrain so she'd know where she landed and how far she'd have to hike to a road. The lower she got, the less she could see anything except the tops of trees. She aimed her wing toward what looked like the open area of a hiking trail. It was tight. On Mount Garfield, she guessed. She S turned over the landing zone to lose altitude. She was coming straight down. The zone was too small. The left side of her wing collapsed, turning her to the right. It reinflated but snagged a tree branch, sending her into a fast spin. She swung out under the wing and hit the ground, hard on her right hip. Pain shot through her like a contraction of childbirth, then subsided into the exhausting ache that came between contractions.

She rolled onto her left side, took off her helmet, and

unclipped her harness, managing to free herself enough that she could sit up. The wing lay as deflated as a carnival balloon in front of her, its edge torn. Her right side hurt from her ribs to her feet. She propped herself on her left elbow to look at the GPS that was clipped onto the front of the harness. Nothing showed. She remembered the low battery. She tried to radio Phil. No response from anyone on the frequency. She took her cell phone out of her jacket pocket. The clock read 2:12. No bars. She needed to call Mark. Her best option was to start down the trail and hope for a hiker to come by.

Keeping her legs stretched forward, she reached behind her. The twisting sent a line of pain from her hip to her foot. She pulled her wing toward her and, still resting on her left side, folded it as neatly as she could so it would fit into her pack. She ignored the ripping sound she heard. When she had secured everything, she felt the pain rise to her consciousness. She used her left leg to kick her pack to the edge of the trail, aiming for a tree she could hold onto. She slid on her butt to it. A squirrel ran in front of her, an acorn in its mouth. Above, birds began the kind of squawking they did when a storm was coming. Thunder sounded in the distance. She grabbed the tree with both arms, stood on her left leg, and tried putting her weight onto her right leg. It wouldn't hold her. She'd have to hop down the mountain.

Standing on her left leg, she reached for her pack and got it onto her back. She bent and picked up a large stick to use as a hiking pole. She managed a dozen hops before she admitted that she couldn't get down the mountain that way. She sat, legs straight in front of her, then lifted her right foot over the ankle of her left leg to keep the pressure off her injured hip. After a few minutes of butt sliding, she knew she'd never make it down the mountain with her pack. She unclipped it and left it in the middle of the trail. Maybe someone would find it and return $10,000 worth of equipment.

The rain started. The canopy of trees sheltered her from the worst of it and the thunder stayed far enough away that she knew the lightning wasn't close. She slid and rested, slid and rested, her progress as agonizing as the pain. She checked her cell phone again. 3:32 and still no bars. By then the thunder had stopped and the rain had moderated, tempting her to lie down and let the mountain take her. She looked at her phone again. 4:13 and no bars. She heard a rumble, a car, not thunder. She'd make it. She tried to think what road she'd come out on. Maybe Route 3. When she reached the bottom, she saw that the road was dirt, one of the offshoots that got hikers to the trailhead.

She sat so close to the road that she risked being hit by a car. She wished she had her brightly colored wing to throw over her. Free of the effort of sliding and wet through from the rain, she was freezing. She butt-slid to the shelter of a tree that hadn't dropped all its leaves. Most of the fall colors would be gone by morning, the leaves fertilizer for the earth. She unzipped her pocket and looked at her phone again. One bar. She pressed Mark's number. She pointed the phone's flashlight to the sign that marked the trailhead. Garfield Trail, 4.7 miles.

Mark answered on the first ring. "Monica. Thought you'd get down early. "I've been waiting for your call ever since the storm hit."

"I crashed."

The call disconnected. A blue truck drove by. She flashed her phone. The truck slowed enough that the driver should have seen her. He looked like he might be the waiter from The Bethlehem Inn. He drove on. She called Mark again. This time he answered with a question. "Where are you?"

"I'm freezing under a tree at the Mount Garfield trailhead."

"I'll find it. Twenty minutes." He hung up.

She tried to stop her shivering by breathing into her pain. Each breath rose and became a different image. The reds and oranges of her wing transposing into the limbs of trees. A hung-over waiter floating above her table. Sierra becoming Jenny. Jenny becoming Phil the paraglider, lying on snowpack with rain pouring over him.

She heard a car or truck on the gravel, coming fast. Before she could see it, she began flashing the light from her phone up and down the road. When it came into view, she could see that it was Mark's SUV.

Mark stepped out of the car and stood with his feet just in front of where she had stretched her legs out. His boots still looked clean. He crouched next to her. "What hurts?"

"My hip. The right one." She gasped when he pressed

hard against it. He pressed all down her leg then onto her hip again, harder this time. "Is it broken?" she managed to say.

"Could be." He pressed again.

The blue truck returned down the road. The driver stopped, rolled down his window. Monica could see him. The waiter from the inn.

"Film," he said. "Everything okay?"

"We're good, Bobby."

The waiter drove away.

Mark moved so his knee dug into Monica's shoulder. "That's Bobby Cocoran. He was on the ski team. Younger than us. Not as good as I was. Before you ruined my life."

Monica looked through the glare of the car light onto Mark's face. She saw the sharp, blue eyes that once made him movie star handsome. He looked unhinged. "You're Film?" The wiry athlete had gained bulk, gone gray, unrecognizable behind glasses and a beard.

"You've changed," said Monica, fear rising above the pain in her hip.

"I knew you right away," he said. "At the gas station. Waited for you at Cannon. You made it so easy."

"Why didn't you tell me then who you are?"

"Planned to drink with you. Tell you how you ruined my life. Leave you with the bill to stew in your beer. Or whatever cocktail you drink." He ground his leg into her shoulder. "This is so much better."

"I haven't seen you since high school. Why are you hurting me?"

"You ruined my life when you killed Jenny." For the third time he spat out the word "ruined."

"I didn't kill Jenny. She fell against that tree."

"And you just skied away while I saw Jenny lying there with blood pouring from her face onto the snow. Never could race after that. Every slalom pole looked like a tree. Every race, I saw my own blood on the mountain."

She saw Film racing through the slalom poles, seconds ahead of everyone. All the aggression he once used for skiing was directed toward her. "You were so good."

"No point in skiing when I knew I wouldn't make the Olympics. I could have, you know. Could have been Cannon's Bode Miller. You destroyed all that."

"It's not my fault."

"I saw you cut her off. Admit it."

She dug deep to find the guilt she had buried at Jenny's funeral. Saw Jenny traversing the icy slope. Saw herself waving to Film, telling him to follow her down the mountain, to leave Jenny behind.

Film rose from his crouch. He pulled her farther into the woods, reached for her cell phone, and dropped it on the ground. "I'm leaving you the way you left Jenny. I'll tell Bobby to get you. Tomorrow. Let you lie here the way you left Jenny lying on Hardscrabble."

"Please, Film. Don't leave me here." She remembered leaving Jenny, seeing her lying on the trail, knowing she was hurt. She remembered laughing, remembered the moment of disappointment when Film didn't follow her down the mountain. She watched Film's once-lithe body stagger forward, a hiking boot, wet and not yet broken in, smashing her phone and disappearing. She heard his car start and pull away.

"I'm sorry," she said. Only the trees were listening.

Pavlov's Puppies

MISS ELLEN STOCKWELL was one of our own. The smartest kid who ever went through Deerborn Elementary School, my father used to tell me. Those days we had only an elementary school and when Ellen graduated from high school the next town over, people weren't surprised that she disappeared. She left permanently, they thought, to work and study with "foreign intellectu'ls." But roots run deep in New Hampshire's north country, and a few years later, Ellen returned from a rumored apprenticeship at the Pavlov Institute. She appeared one day at the bus station, suitcase in one hand, a small girl-child in the other.

No one knew where the girl-child came from, but she had the curliest, reddest hair this side of Concord. Even Ellen's widowed father must not have known, for he alone among the Stockwells had been a talking man. People speculated about an abandoned lover or a patient at the Pavlov Institute who had fathered the child before he lapsed into permanent schizophrenia. Deerborn is not a prying town, so no one asked even a year later, when the child and Ellen's father both died of the same unexplained malady of the nervous system.

Ellen was left, the only surviving Stockwell, the owner of a steadily declining house on Stockwell Hill just down from the elementary school. She became Miss Ellen, hired to teach alongside the aging Miss Jansen, who may have frowned upon the young teacher's newfangled ideas, but hadn't energy to protest.

We were eleven children in Miss Ellen's class, the beginning of a booming generation of war babies. Stacey Grant, an undersized first grader, sat next to me all that overwhelming fall when I was learning that school meant more than reading and writing. Stacey never appeared for recess. She stayed inside for what Miss Ellen called special help and what we thought connected somehow to her motherless childhood. Joe Grant never allowed his only child, born of a protracted labor that killed her mother, to mix with the other children. I would study her frail body, her drifting eyes, her mouth that would go slack when she wasn't mumbling. But she remained for me as much an enigma as Miss Ellen.

What Miss Ellen would do with her during recess time we never knew, and when the school board called all of us in to "explain about Miss Ellen and Stacey Grant," we had nothing to tell except that if she started to moan in class, Miss Ellen would ring a little bell and the moaning would stop. She never called on Stacey or put her in a reading group or had her do the morning jumping jacks. But she didn't ignore her either. Every time we'd change from arithmetic to reading or from reading to art projects, she'd first attend to Stacey. She'd give her a piece of paper and a crayon, or the beaded abacus, or any of her drawerful of assorted and mysterious objects that looked like two-piece puzzles. Stacey could never fit the pieces together any more than she could draw with the crayons or make sense of the abacus.

Perhaps the first thing we learned, the thing I most remember, was Miss Ellen kneeling next to Stacey's desk, her soft blond hair even with Stacey's red braids, her thin, pale hands placing a crayon or puzzle or the abacus into Stacey's uncontrolled grasp. Then she would ring her little bell, rise, begin our lesson in a voice too strong for her thin body, and Stacey would stay quiet. Until one day after we'd faced the school board, Stacey was gone.

Miss Ellen remained just a month longer, a month I remember as filled with oddities and the ever-present bell. Every morning she would take out paper and pencil and books and give us some vague sort of instructions. As soon as recess came, she would ask me to be Pavlov's puppy, a term she uttered with hushed wonder. She would take me into the closet, sit me on her lap, and stroke the ponytail that tried to tame my thick red hair. Then she would read from a great book of fairy tales that lived the rest of the day on a shelf in back of the schoolroom.

When she finished a story, she would take me off her lap and stand me in front of her. She would ask me to retell the story. If I summarized poorly, she would turn out the light. If I recited well, she would ring the bell and give me a piece of candy out of a tin with a picture of a fruit on the lid. Over and over for what must have been a month, Miss Ellen led me through the game, the times I performed well lengthening each day. I remember it not as unpleasant but as confusing and very tiring and as a ravenous hunger for the little pieces of candy. For years, I dreamed about fairy tales, but their contents would fade when I woke up, leaving a longing I can only describe as an emptiness like the one I feel when there's a holiday and I have no place to go.

On the last day, the police came and I was pulled from the closet before recess ended. Miss Ellen never returned to the school, almost never emerged from her house, and never called on anyone to keep that house in any kind of repair. Gradually she became known as the town eccentric, the woman children were afraid of, the one adults left to her peace. The one I could not forget.

I have lived for years now, alone in a neat, tiny house next to Miss Ellen's on Stockwell Hill. I have watched the children quicken their pace and hunch their shoulders as they rush past her house. It isn't one of the oldest houses in Deerborn, but, built before 1900, it should have been respectably old. Instead, it stands like a cancer next to the sidewalk, its paint chipping, its shutters askew, its half-drawn shades obscuring the darkness within. No window is ever battened down to keep out the January winds or opened on the hottest dog days of summer. No one sweeps the cluttered porch that covers a full side of the house.

In summer, the house smells vaguely of the skunk that lives somewhere in the overgrown yard. Even in January, the porch smells of dampness and rot, not the rancid smell of decaying garbage, but the musty smell of wet newspapers and cardboard boxes.

I began to notice a change in January that soon became obvious to others. Old rumors surfaced from sixty years of silence. Though she was in her nineties, Miss Ellen could still walk the quarter mile to the village where she bought her boxes and bags of dried food and begged a jug of water and a day-old newspaper. Before the children were freed from school, she would be back in that house, cocooned beneath a nest of blankets and newspapers—we never believed she read those day old papers—in the lone back room that sometimes was lighted by an oil lamp.

It was this burning lamp that first signaled the change. From my bedroom window, I could see it lighting up the back room until after ten o'clock, though it was the coldest time of the year so that in her heatless house Miss Ellen should long ago have nested down. January was the month when ordinarily the lamp burned least often, Miss Ellen's nighttime hours increasing in direct proportion with the decreasing hours of sunlight. I often thought that only her south-facing window kept her from perishing during the cold winter.

The first night I noticed the lamp, I thought Miss Ellen must have fallen asleep and I prepared to keep an all night vigil for fear the house and its papers would ignite. But before midnight the lamp stopped burning, and I went to bed more puzzled than relieved. The next night, the lamp burned again. By the third night, I knew that Miss Ellen was not falling asleep, and by the end of the week, the rumors had begun. Each day when Miss Ellen begged water for her plumbing-less house, she bought a little tin of French hard candies made without artificial color, a fruit design on each lid signaling the flavor within.

Along with the fruited candies, we began to see Vera talking to her. Vera was the daughter of a middle-aged widower, who had long ago lost all control of her. The villagers kept one wary eye on her and with the other ignored which of the town toughs were hanging around her. Gradually, Vera began to appear every day at Miss Ellen's. Each night, I heard the soft, high tinkle of a bell.

As winter passed and the weather began to soften, Vera and Miss Ellen would emerge from the house together, Vera's body seeming to fatten in direct proportion to how Miss Ellen's dissolved. On the warmest days they would sit on the step of the porch while the sun was high. We began to joke about how with her red hair, Vera could have been a teenaged incarnation of Miss Ellen's dead child. But eventually we ignored them, taking them out only once in awhile for a piece of local color to share with visitors.

That spring the gypsy moths invaded, covering our trees and lawns and driveways in masses of brown caterpillars. At night we could hear them munching through the new greenery and in the morning we would sweep away their droppings, using cleanliness as a battle tactic. Except for

Miss Ellen whose house the caterpillars chose to cover, or perhaps whose house they retreated to when we swept them away from our own. Soon they transformed the cracking, dirty white clapboards into brown undulations, a moving sea of infestation that seemed nourished more by the house's decay than by the emerging leaves of the tree in front of it. They crept through the cracks in the front door and through torn plastic that covered the broken windows. We began to see them crawling along the insides of the shades and curtains.

The porch was a breeding ground. Children were instructed to cross the street before they walked past Miss Ellen's house. Parents called the school, which called the county health department, which assured us all that unless we let them crawl on us, gypsy moths were harmless and would naturally kill themselves off with their own gluttony. So we swept and we scrubbed, and shuddered when Miss Ellen walked through her porch without brushing a path for herself. Even Vera knew enough to push aside caterpillars. One day I watched her walk behind Miss Ellen delicately picking them off the back of a skirt I recognized as one I had put in the recycle box outside the village store.

Toward the end of the infestation, when we could walk outside in the morning without sweeping away square gypsy moth droppings, Vera came from Miss Ellen's house alone. She looked haggard, as spent as the dying gypsy moths. She spoke to no one and even her father didn't know why she left town or where she had gone.

After five days when Miss Ellen hadn't appeared for her supply of groceries and newspapers, I called the police chief, who called the ambulance squad to follow him into the house. They parked on the edge of the sidewalk, lights flashing in anticipation of what we knew they would find. A Deerborn crowd gathered to watch as they climbed to the porch.

I saw the skunk I had known must be living off Miss Ellen's debris. It dove under what looked like an old hassock, its fur blending with the hassock's spilling insides. The porch was covered with dead or dying caterpillars, a few that had managed to metamorphose to the moth stage resting in a tight group on a plastic bag caught on the edge of a torn screen. I could smell death, like a pile of sweaty clothes thrown against a radiator and cooked, the body odor putrefying as the sweat dried. No one stopped me when I followed them inside.

Miss Ellen must have been dead the whole week. She lay on top of a ragged blanket, curled in a fetal ball in a darkened corner. My skirt was tangled around her hips, revealing bare legs covered with the dried ooze of sores. Two hatched moths moved along her body, nibbling the fabric of her clothes. Trailing down her back was her blond hair, darkened with dirt and age. I saw the hair move, and move again, and again, alive with nesting caterpillars.

A tiny baby lay in her arms, naked and red, its umbilical cord wrapped around its neck.

Next to the shriveled bodies, I saw the supplies of the schoolroom I remembered so well. The book of fairy tales, the candy, the little bell. I picked up the bell and heard its same sharp tinkle. Beneath it lay a diary. I opened it to the last page. "Vera will give me back my child. She will be the last."

I closed the diary, put it in my pocket, and reached for the book, the bell, and the tin of candy.

I rarely go out now. I watch the changing seasons wrap themselves around the house on Stockwell Hill. I read the fairy tales I remember so well. I recite the stories. When I take a recess from my work, I ring the little bell and eat a piece of candy.

The Man Who Loved Cribbage

An aged man is but a paltry thing,
A tattered coat upon a stick, unless
Soul clap its hands and sing, and louder sing
For every tatter in its mortal dress...
                              —William Butler Yeats

THE OLD MAN lived off the grid in a shack he had built himself. It lay hidden from the road along a curve in the river, nearly invisible to anyone driving by. He dug his own well, put rain collectors under his gutter, and cut wood for his fireplace and his cookstove. Long before the alternative energy movement, he used the current of the river to rig up a system that provided him the little electricity he required. He rose with the light and, except for Fridays when he played cribbage with Moses Flannery, he never turned on a lamp. Moses was one of the few left in town who had known Old Man Hanrahan before he went off to college and came back, forty-five years later, an eccentric. For a time, people called him the mad man in the shack and circulated rumors that he had been locked up in the state hospital in Concord. After a few months when he hadn't come into the village talking to an invisible companion or wandering under a full moon in a night shirt, they speculated that he had been a spy or a mercenary, or he had invented some top secret government weapon and retreated from the world in shame. He had a car, he bought gas and groceries, he had money even if he didn't spend much.

Hazel Foster knew more about Old Man Hanrahan and those cribbage games than anyone except Moses, but she didn't know much. She was never invited into the shack during the year she drove Moses to the games and Moses and Old Man Hanrahan to the grocery store. She was a healthy eighty-four, still able to drive, when the men hit ninety and failed the New Hampshire driving test. Moses walked across the street from his house to hers and asked if she'd accept twenty dollars a week to be their chauffeur. She would have driven for nothing.

Hazel had been watching Old Man Hanrahan since she was in elementary school and he was Jimmy Hanrahan, a teenager in the one school building that housed the town's hundred or so children, first grade through twelfth. He stood out then, a little curved in the spine, with thick dark hair that he wore too long on the sides for the high and tight style of post-World War II America. He lived a half-mile beyond her house and walked the same route to school. Most days, he jostled with Moses as they passed her. If he walked alone, she'd make up stories about why he was kicking stones or hitting trees with a stick he'd picked up along the road. She liked best the days he was late. She'd hear him coming up behind her and stand still for a moment, waiting. He'd stop and pat her on the head. If it was warm, he'd say, "Hey, Shirley Temple, curls look mighty fine today." If she wore a hat against the cold of winter, he'd pull it off as he ran past her, then stop, and put it back on her head, being careful to cover her ears. He'd run his finger along her nose and, without saying anything, continue on his way.

Hazel liked walking to school alone. She liked to walk slowly, pretending to be Nancy Drew looking along the road for clues to who had been visiting Mrs. Drake while her husband was away, who had poisoned Mr. Fletcher's horse, who had committed whatever theft or murder her eleven-year-old mind could imagine. Often, she'd imagine stories about Jimmy Hanrahan. Someone put a snake in his locker and she saw the remnants of a snake skin on Moses' jacket. Someone had stolen Jimmy's English paper and she stayed after school, snuck up the stairs to the high school rooms, and found it in Moses' desk. Jimmy wasn't always the victim. Often he was her partner in the H & J Detective Agency.

When Jimmy graduated and left her, a bereft seventh grader, she imagined him at the state university studying a science he could use to help her solve crimes. The first Christmas Jimmy returned to Lakeview, he told her he was majoring in electrical engineering. It sounded important, something that would be useful for their detective agency. He still joked about her Shirley Temple hair, still ran his finger along her nose, still wore his hair a little too long, but he had changed in a way she didn't understand. By the next year when he hadn't come home from college for the summer, she heard rumors that he had dropped out of school, gone to Europe or enlisted in the navy. From then on, she tried to forget about Jimmy Hanrahan.

She graduated from high school, the valedictorian, which didn't mean much in a class of eight, but she was smart enough to get into the university and do well. In college, she stayed in the background, observing how the young women in spring would exchange pleated skirts and knee socks for petticoated dresses, and the men with their crew-cuts would take off their letter sweaters and sit in the sun on the library steps. If she walked by and one of the men called out that he liked her curly hair, she'd rub her finger along her nose and think of Jimmy Hanrahan.

Hazel made friends among the women who went to college in the 1950s to learn, not to look for a husband. She dated a few men who took her to the movies or a football game or dances hosted by the university. Once she ended up at a fraternity party where people drank from a bowl of punch concocted of fruit juice, ginger ale, and alcohol distilled by the chemistry majors in their lab. They called it rocket fuel. After she had drunk her third glass, she collapsed into her date's arms while the band played "Ebb Tide." He half-carried her back to her dorm where she woke the next morning with a hangover that turned her off alcohol forever.

She graduated *magna cum laude*, returned home to Lakeview still a virgin. There she remained a virgin, committed to imagining rather than living life. She inherited her parents' house, across the street from the house where Moses grew up and which he had never left. Although he hadn't gone to university, he made a good life for himself as a local carpenter. It was Moses who helped Jimmy Hanrahan build what the town nicknamed Jimmy's Folly.

While they were building, Jimmy lived with Moses. At first, Hazel would stop over in the evening, offering a pie or a fresh loaf of bread. She'd say, "How's the building going?" and Moses would say, "Coming along." Each visit, she'd try out a new angle to solve the mystery of Jimmy Hanrahan. "Do you find Lakeview changed? Different from where you were living?" "Where'd you learn to build houses?" "How'd you make the money to buy all those materials?" Jimmy would look up from whatever book he was reading, shake his head, then bend it to the book again. Moses would say, "Jimmy's earned his privacy." Finally, Hazel had to accept that, like everyone else in town, she could only wonder.

For the next twenty-seven years, Jimmy welcomed no one into his shack except Moses for their Friday cribbage games. If Moses knew what had happened to him, he kept it as secret as Jimmy did. People who had gone to school with Jimmy died or moved away and along with them their knowing glances. Jimmy became Old Man Hanrahan, a recluse best left alone.

Jimmy hadn't spoken to Hazel even once during those twenty-seven years. Her Shirley Temple curls had thinned to a dry gray and her eyebrows had disappeared along with most of her body hair. Until she hit eighty, she walked every day, even when the New Hampshire weather turned to a cold as biting as her curious eyes. Passing what had been the town's only school and that now housed administrative offices, she'd start up the dirt road beyond it and walk toward the river where Jimmy had built his shack. The road ended at a boat ramp where she'd turn around and retrace her steps. At eighty, she gave in to age, parked at the boat ramp, and walked two miles instead of five, reducing her days to Wednesdays and Saturdays. Occasionally when she passed Jimmy's Folly, she'd see him at his mailbox. He'd look at her, smile, and run his finger along his nose.

One morning when she had just turned seventy, the sun sparkled on a layer of fresh snow, reminding her of all the winter mornings she walked to school imagining stories about Jimmy Hanrahan. She passed Jimmy in front of his mailbox. Perhaps it was an impulse carved as deep as the snow into his memory that moved him to the gesture. He snatched off her hat, tossed it in the air and, laughing, handed it back to her.

The pressure of his hand, the familiar flick of his

wrist, reawakened the creativity that produced a novel she wrote after college. Its success shocked her. *Hard Soil* had done for rural New Hampshire in the 1950s what *To Kill a Mockingbird* had done for 1930s Mississippi. Her characters were taciturn, some would say hard like the soil. She captured the smoldering resentments between families, but also the way they banded together when a wolf came to someone's door. She looked behind closed doors and showed her readers that however dreadful their lives, New Englanders never aired their dirty secrets in public. She had gone on the book tour, consented to radio interviews that terrified her, then retreated to privacy in a town that protected her from the occasional reporter who wanted to know if she had more novels waiting to be published. *Hard Soil* continued to sell, mostly to college classes on New England literature, enough copies that she could live the simple life she enjoyed. She had some handwritten manuscripts filed away, but the story that still nagged her was the one she couldn't imagine. Why had Jimmy Hanrahan disappeared and why had he returned to live off the grid, his only company Moses Flannery?

It was nearly a decade and a half after Jimmy had snatched away her hat before Moses knocked on her door and offered her the twenty dollars. She, like the rest of the town, had begun to think of Jimmy as Old Man Hanrahan. She rarely saw him now and with each sighting he had become a little more stooped. When Moses approached her to become a driver for two old men, she bought a package of twelve legal pads, a half-dozen of the pens she still used to compose a first draft, and replenished her supply of ink cartridges and paper for the book she would at last write.

On the first Monday, she parked her car in Moses' driveway, got out and looked at the placard over the front porch that announced the date of the house. 1848. It felt as old as Old Man Hanrahan, but it had weathered the years better. Every summer, Moses would replace clapboards or fix a porch railing. He weeded the flower garden that his mother had nursed into a spectacular display and that his wife had tended until childbirth killed her. The perennials still bloomed in a sequence guaranteed to have color from early spring into the late fall when the chrysanthemums gave in to the hard frost that came after the last bloomings of Indian summer.

Now in late October on a morning as bright as a day in June, Hazel imagined a new beginning, the years to come unfolding the story of Jimmy Hanrahan. Moses opened the door before she had a chance to ring the bell. He wore a short-sleeved shirt and jeans that sat high on his waist, belted just a little too tight. His arms that once rippled with muscles toned from carpentry had gone slack and his once thick hair had vanished, revealing a bald scalp freckled by the sun.

"Come inside, Hazel," he said through thin lips on a face that bore the deep lines of a life spent outdoors. "Just finishing my coffee. Offer you a cup?"

"Already had mine," said Hazel.

"I'll just get my coat then."

She stepped into a living room that hadn't changed since

the days she and Moses were kids. Except for the heat that explained his short-sleeved shirt. The temperature was cranked as high as a smoldering day in summer.

The walls held the same paintings Hazel remembered from her childhood when she thought Mrs. Flannery must be one of the best artists in the world. They were oils, scenes of the town's school, the ballpark, the lake the town had been named for, the curve in the river where Jimmy had built his shack, all recognizable, all stiff and a little off-kilter. The one window that opened onto the porch was still framed with the curtains Hazel had helped sew after Moses' mother died and his wife felt free to put her own touches into the house. When his wife tried to take down the paintings, Moses had threatened her with divorce, so on the walls they remained. The curtains were as faded now as the sofa that faced the fireplace and the mantel that held photos of Moses' father, one in his wedding suit in front of the house where he brought his bride and one in the uniform of the war that turned him into a paraplegic, dead before Moses reached puberty. Another photo showed Moses' mother posed in her wedding gown, a sleek, cream-colored satin with a high beaded neck, cap sleeves, and belted waist. The skirt fell only to mid-calf, revealing stockings in shoes that buttoned at the ankle. The only photo of Moses' wife showed her in a chair, visibly pregnant and knitting a blanket for the child who died with her minutes after his birth. Hazel remembered that week, the way the town had gathered around Moses, the way he fought off sorrow by building his wife's coffin, the way he built a life by becoming known as the best carpenter in a hundred mile radius.

Only when Jimmy Hanrahan returned decades later did Moses recover the joy that showed in the last photograph on the mantel. It was of him and Jimmy, posed as bare-chested teenagers, their arms around each other at the boat ramp. When Moses came back into the living room, the sight of him zipping a slightly soiled ski parka shocked Hazel into remembering that he was an old man and that Jimmy had long ago become Old Man Hanrahan.

Moses held out a ten dollar bill that Hazel tucked into her pocket. He reached for a wool cap resting on top of a coat rack next to the front door, opened the door for her, and only when he stepped outside put it onto his bald head. He brushed away her arm when she offered it, standing tall as he descended the steps that led off the porch to the walkway.

"Can't see enough to drive," he said, "but I'm still steady on my feet."

"Hope I'm as fit as you when I reach ninety," said Hazel.

"You're not so far behind."

"Just six years."

Moses opened the car door for Hazel, gave a little bow, and seemed to pull himself up taller as he walked to the passenger side. He slid in, found the lever, and moved the seat back to accommodate his long legs.

"Sorry," said Hazel. "I'll be sure to have the seat pushed back next time."

"No matter."

Hazel started the car. After she had safely backed out of the driveway, she said, "How's Jimmy? I worry about him. He looks more stooped every time I see him at his mailbox."

"Got the arthritis pretty bad. Okay 'cept for that."

"Does he have help around the house? Someone to do his laundry?" Hazel wondered if she could add house cleaner to taxi driver.

"Don't need help. He's stronger than he looks."

Hazel ventured further. "Who cuts his wood?"

"Does it himself." Moses turned his face to the window. "Pretty day out."

They passed the building where they had gone to school so long ago. "Seems like we were just kids walking to school," Hazel said.

Moses stayed silent. He'd said enough. Hazel turned onto the river road. After the first half mile, the pavement changed to dirt and dirt it remained until it dead-ended at the boat ramp. Except in summer when fishermen launched their rowboats and couples went out in canoes, it was the road less traveled. Every summer someone would come back with a story about Old Man Hanrahan. He'd shouted at them not to fish in front of his house, he'd been chopping wood and raised a threatening ax, he'd fallen asleep on a boulder, his chin resting on his fist so he looked like The Thinker. Some swore he lived with a woman and claimed they saw her throwing stones into the river. If young boys caught him peeing in the bushes, they'd make jokes about shriveled penises that had never been used.

Hazel put on her blinker at Jimmy's mailbox though there were no cars in sight. She pulled into the driveway and turned off the ignition. "No need to get out of the car," she said.

"You either," said Moses. "Jimmy'll see us."

Hazel opened the car door anyway. "I'll just see if he needs help." She heard Moses mumble something that sounded like "nosy as ever" when she stepped onto the packed dirt that passed for Jimmy's driveway. She had never been this close to the house. The townspeople who called it a shack were right. It was no bigger than an oversized storage shed, its clapboards unpainted and so weathered it was nearly hidden among trees that would keep it cool in summer and turn it into an animal's den in winter. If she didn't know about the cribbage games, she would have believed that Jimmy hibernated with the bears that still roamed the woods in Lakeview. Anemic smoke rose from a metal chimney. Enough logs to keep Jimmy all winter were stacked neatly between posts on the side of the house. Hazel counted three cleared or recovering areas that marked each decade Jimmy cut wood so he could live off the grid. The morning sun shone on a vegetable garden close to the river, fenced off from the deer, the woodchucks, and the raccoons that anyone who tried to grow a garden in Lakeview wanted to annihilate. Only a sad-looking row of kale hadn't been harvested.

Jimmy was standing in front of a door as weathered as the clapboards. It was closed and the window curtains were drawn. Hazel hadn't been this close to Jimmy since the day he pulled off her hat. He had never been tall, but now his stoop had shortened him to her five and a half feet. He looked shrunken beneath a parka designed in the 1980s, short and puffy, its gray now faded to a silver sheen. Beneath it, she could see a belt holding up pants that were as old as the jacket and worn at the knees. Deep furrows lined his face, and his eyes looked at her under eyebrows as thick as his hair, gray now and still long on the sides. He reached into his pocket, pulled out a ten dollar bill, and handed it to her. She wished she had taken off her gloves so she could feel the skin of his blue-veined hands.

"Much obliged," he said, walking in front of her to the car. He got into the back seat beside Moses, who had moved from the front and had left the back door open for him.

"Morning," Moses said. Jimmy nodded his response.

Hazel started the car, watching the two men in her rearview mirror. In their tattered coats, they looked like the aged men of the Yeats' poem she had studied in college. Paltry things, but familiar to each other, even companionable.

"Gotten over your beating Friday?" said Moses. "Ready for a rematch?"

"Blind luck drawing the right Jack for three cribs."

"Strategy," said Moses.

"Luck and probability," said Jimmy.

"And knowing when to dump the lone Jack."

"Or use Old Faithful." Jimmy leaned toward Hazel in the driver's seat. "Just talkin' about cribbage. Mostly all we talk about."

Hazel hadn't heard Jimmy speak in the years he had lived in his shack. The high tone of his voice had turned raspy with age, but it still carried the hint of something withheld that she used to imagine she'd learn when they were grown. By the time she pulled into the parking lot of the grocery store, she began to think that Jimmy was simply Old Man Hanrahan, a recluse with only one friend, with only one interest in life, with nothing to fill the pages of her twelve legal pads.

Inside the store, the two men walked, Moses behind Jimmy, up and down each of the aisles. Hazel was more interested in watching what Jimmy bought than what she put into her own cart. After they had gone through every aisle, she found a check-out counter where she could see Jimmy at the register next to hers. He leaned on his cart, so hunched that a toddler riding the cart behind him asked her mother if he was a gnome. The mother shushed her, saying that gnomes were just pretend. Jimmy turned and when he saw the little girl's hair, said, "You look like Shirley Temple." He looked at Hazel and ran his finger along his nose. Behind her, Moses said, "He never forgets the old days."

Jimmy unloaded the meager contents of his cart. Nothing that required a freezer. Pasta and sauce, milk and eggs, enough bananas to make Hazel wonder if he had a potassium deficiency. He bought no meat and only a single head of lettuce. She imagined he was a vegetarian living off vegetables he stored in a root cellar. He paid with a credit card. On the way out, he stopped to withdraw money from an ATM. She strained to read the screen. He was being charged $3.00 for using a bank different from his own. Available funds, $140,076 and some amount of change she couldn't read. She thought of her own checking account and its balance of a few thousand dollars. Did Jimmy keep all his money in a checking account? She remembered the long ago rumors about him working on a secret military project or being a government spy. Wherever he got however much money he had, he had learned how to access it without going to a local bank.

He counted the bills that shot out of the ATM and looked at his receipt. "Seen what you wanted?" he said, as he put the card into the pocket of his jacket and pushed his cart to Hazel's car. She opened the trunk and loaded in five bags of groceries, one for herself and two each for Moses and Jimmy.

The conversation on the drive back returned to cribbage and who won Crusty's One Day in Portsmouth. Moses explained to Hazel, "I follow all the local tournaments. Fill Jimmy in. He refuses to get a computer."

"Or a phone," said Jimmy. "Like my privacy."

"Or multiple bank accounts?" Hazel said. She wanted to know if Jimmy kept his privacy by avoiding more than one account.

"Leave him be," said Moses.

Hazel said nothing else until they reached Jimmy's shack. She got out of the car, opened her trunk, and picked up both of Jimmy's bags. Before he managed to get out of the car, she reached the door to his house, set down the bags and turned the knob to go inside. Jimmy came up beside her. "Locked. Sometimes I remember. Go now. I can still carry my own groceries." He took a key out of the pocket of his jacket. The ATM card fell out. Hazel picked it up and handed it back. It was a Wells Fargo card, a bank that had no branches in northern New England. Only when she got back into her car did she see him put the key into the lock, pick up his groceries, and go inside.

Moses had returned to the front seat. "Don't push Jimmy," he said. "He don't confide in anyone."

"Not even you?" said Hazel.

"Not to be told, not to be told."

Hazel drove Moses and Jimmy every Monday for a year. She rarely thought of Jimmy now as anyone other than Old Man Hanrahan. Although his back became so stooped it was bent nearly into an L, he still carried his own grocery bags. Every Monday she heard the same conversations about cribbage strategy. She read up on the rules and the strategies so she understood the basics of what the crib was, what it meant to peg out, even knew terms like "two for his heels" and "his nob." Once, she offered to join Jimmy and Moses in their games. They met her offer with silence.

Every Friday, she dropped Moses at Jimmy's and picked him up after their games. He revealed nothing more than their statistics for game wins in a technical jargon she never quite understood. As much as she strained to see inside the shack, the curtains remained drawn, the door opening only for the seconds it took for Moses to step inside.

Eventually, a Monday came when Moses called her to say he was ill. Jimmy would expect him so she should drive to his place. He doubted that Jimmy would go to the grocery store without him. She opened her back door to check the weather. Cool and clear, promising to warm into the kind of June day that reminded people of why they lived in New Hampshire. She fixed a bowl of oatmeal laced with a combination of seeds and a banana, the kind of breakfast that had kept her healthy for eighty-five years. Her biggest concession to modernity besides a computer and a cell phone was the Keurig coffee maker that saved her from throwing out the dregs of coffee she used to keep too long after making a pot. Some changes were good, she told herself.

She finished her breakfast, washed her dishes by hand, and laid out a pair of lightweight pants and a cotton blouse with sleeves long enough to hide her wrinkled skin. When she went into the bathroom to wash herself and comb her hair, the mirror told her that Jimmy wouldn't remember her as the young girl with the Shirley Temple curls. She found her purse and her car keys. Before she left, she unwrapped the package of legal pads, setting one on her desk, a pen beside it. She imagined a title for what she'd write. *The Lady and the Old Man: A History of Love.*

On the drive to Jimmy's, she thought of ways to talk herself inside. Someone had left a package at his mailbox, he dropped his hat in his garden, Moses had sent a new deck of cards. None gave her a solution for what to do when she went inside and had no package, no hat, no cards. The only excuse she could think of was to say she needed to use his bathroom.

She pulled onto the hard dirt of the driveway and turned off the ignition. She looked at her face in the rearview mirror, pushing a gray strand away from her forehead. When she got out of the car, she stood as tall as her eighty-five years would allow and adjusted her blouse. In her head, she was a schoolgirl again.

When no Jimmy stood at the door, her anticipation turned to worry. Was he, like Moses, ill? She knocked, waited, knocked again. When he still didn't answer, she touched the doorknob. It turned and the door opened.

Enough light shone through the drawn curtains so that, stepping inside, she could see the spartan interior. A kitchen area to the right with a sink, a small refrigerator, an apartment sized stove. A pan and a couple of dishes lay in a drainer next to the sink. A table with two chairs stood in the middle of the single room. She assumed that the two closed doors led to a bedroom and a bathroom.

"Jimmy, are you home?" she called.

No one answered. She pulled aside a curtain. Light shone through a cloud of dust motes onto the table. Four pegs were lined up in the start position on a cribbage board, handcrafted from a curved oak branch. A deck of cards lay in the center of the table, cut to show the Queen of Hearts. A worn brown leather notebook lay beside it. She picked it up and paged through lists of dates, scores, significant plays. Two columns at the top of each page spelled out the names: Moses and Shirley.

Puzzled, she called again, "Jimmy?" When he still didn't answer, she moved to the closest door and opened it. A windowless bathroom. She closed that door and opened the one next to it, stepping into Jimmy's bedroom, which was bathed in light from an open window where the curtains had been pulled back.

A woman with light brown curls half-sat, half-lay, slumped against a mound of pillows on the bed. She moved closer. Jimmy's eyes stared unblinking beneath shaggy eyebrows and a wig that had twisted to show strands of gray hair beneath it. His mouth had gone slack and his head drooped to one side.

She found her way into the bathroom, picked up a face cloth hung over the edge of the sink, soaked it in cold water, and held it against her eyes, trying to convince herself that Jimmy wore a wig when he slept to keep himself warm. When her heart rate slowed, she removed the face cloth and saw an old woman, pale and red-eyed, staring back at her.

She went into the kitchen and found a paper bag stored between the refrigerator and the counter. She looked in the refrigerator, empty except for some early lettuce Jimmy must have harvested from his garden. He had only two cupboards, one with a lone box of cereal and an over ripe banana, the other with a few plates and cups. She could see nothing that explained where Jimmy had been for forty-five years, that explained his money, that helped her make sense of the wig. She moved to the table, fingered the cribbage board, then picked up the notebook and put it in the paper bag.

She went back into the bedroom. Jimmy seemed to stare at her, to tell her what she should do. The room had no closet, only a dressing table for Jimmy's clothes. She opened each drawer, finding trousers and shirts, sweaters, the scant evidence of Jimmy's frugal lifestyle. Kneeling to the bottom drawer, she rummaged through socks and underwear. A pair of cotton underpants in little girl pink rested among men's underwear and socks. She put it into the paper bag. She stood up and looked at a double-sided picture frame on the dresser. One side held a picture of the child Shirley Temple wearing a green and white polka dot dress with a Peter Pan collar and baby doll sleeves. It was cut from some long ago magazine.

Hazel closed the frame quickly when she saw herself, a curly-headed six-year-old sitting on Moses' porch. The day Jimmy had taken the photo with a Brownie camera he had gotten for his birthday was the first day she remembered him calling her "Shirley Temple." She put the photo frame into the bag and looked at the pile of clothes next to the dresser. A pair of Mary Jane shoes and white knee socks lay on top of a green and white polka dot dress. She shoved them into the paper bag and turned to the bed where she imagined Jimmy saying, "Thank you."

She pulled down the blanket that covered him. He was naked, his back resting against an indentation worn into the mattress from the L shape of his hunch. His body was as thin now as a little girl's, his penis so small Hazel thought of the boys she overheard talking about shriveled penises that had never been used. She pulled the blanket over Jimmy and knelt beside the bed.

"You could have dressed up for me," she said. "We could have played cribbage together."

She stood up, removed the wig from Jimmy's head, and put it into the paper bag. She ran her finger along his stone-cold nose, bent to kiss his forehead, then walked with the paper bag away from Jimmy's Folly toward the legal pad that would wait empty forever.

Acknowledgments

THANKS GO TO all the people and places that generated these stories. My college roommates for *Six Old Women,* my sister and cousin for "Shuffleboard," my family and friends for "Hardscrabble," my old town in New Hampshire for "Pavlov's Puppies" and "The Man Who Loved Cribbage." Despite their origins, the characters in these stories are imagined, their lives far from the settings and the people I know.

Pathologist and author BJ Magnani, PhD, MD, FCAP (the Dr. Lily Robinson series) gave me the idea for Mad Honey, and Peter Warren helped me with details about paragliding. Authors from Encircle Publications have been wonderful in their support for those of us in the writing game. Special thanks to Encircle's Eddie Vincent, Cynthia Brackett-Vincent, and Deirdre Wait, who look first for good writing when they are considering a book for publication.

As always my Monday Mayhem critique group has

offered sage advice, most of which I follow—Carole Beers (Pepper Kane western mysteries), Clive Rosengren (Eddie Collins LA mysteries), Michael Neimann (International thrillers), and Jenn Ashton (comic mysteries in progress).

Finally and most especially, thank you to my family—Michael, Juliana, Ryan, Emily, Peter, Jasper—who have helped me through this year when I've learned to negotiate widowhood.

"Pavlov's Puppies" was originally published in *Toasted-Cheese*, June 2016.

"The Man Who Loved Cribbage" was originally published in *Permafrost*, 42.2, January 2021.

About the Author

SHARON L. DEAN grew up in Massachusetts where she was immersed in the literature of New England. She earned undergraduate and graduate degrees at the University of New Hampshire, a state she lived and taught in before moving to Oregon. Although she has given up writing scholarly books that require footnotes, she incorporates much of her academic research as background in her mysteries. She is the author of three Susan Warner mysteries, *Tour de Trace*, *Death of the Keynote Speaker*, and *Cemetery Wine*, and of a literary novel titled *Leaving Freedom*. Her Deborah Strong mysteries include *The Barn*, *The Wicked Bible*, and *Calderwood Cove*. Dean continues to write about New England while she is discovering the beauty of the West.